*W*hat

&

Five stars, and Nominee for Sensual Ecataromance Reviewers' Award "The story is full of action and adventure as well as hot sex scenes that will keep the reader glued to the pages of this book. I cannot wait to find out what is next for this clan of vampires." *~ ecataromance*

Five tattoos "I was spellbound...a must read for the vampire lover...I cannot wait for the next installment in this series." *~ Erotic-Escapades Book Reviews*

Five angels "Stefan is an amazing character...a wonderful mix of brooding darkness and vulnerability. Julie is his perfect foil. So understanding and full of life that there was no way that a vampire could resist..." *~ Fallen Angels Reviews*

Five vampires "A fast-moving, action-packed story with tantalizing passion and an honorable vampire that this reader instantly fell for... Ann Jacobs has done a tremendous job at creating not only a series, but a story that readers will want to read more than once and add to their keeper pile. The vampires in this story offer both sides of the spectrum, good and evil, compassionate and bitter, and some of them are to die for." *~ gottawritenetwork.com*

Eternally HIS

d'Argent Honor II

Ann Jacobs

ELLORA'S CAVE
ROMANTICA PUBLISHING

An Ellora's Cave Romantica Publication

www.ellorascave.com

Eternally His

ISBN 1419955993
ALL RIGHTS RESERVED.
Eternally His Copyright © 2006 Ann Jacobs
Edited by Sue-Ellen Gower
Cover art by Syneca

Electronic book Publication March 2006
Trade paperback Publication November 2006

Excerpt from *Dallas Heat* Copyright © Ann Jacobs 2003

Content Advisory:

The following material contains graphic sexual content meant for mature readers. This story has been rated E–rotic by a minimum of three independent reviewers.

Ellora's Cave Publishing offers three levels of Romantica™ reading entertainment: S (S-ensuous), E (E-rotic), and X (X-treme).

S-*ensuous* love scenes are explicit and leave nothing to the imagination.

E-*rotic* love scenes are explicit, leave nothing to the imagination, and are high in volume per the overall word count. In addition, some E-rated titles might contain fantasy material that some readers find objectionable, such as bondage, submission, same sex encounters, forced seductions, and so forth. E-rated titles are the most graphic titles we carry; it is common, for instance, for an author to use words such as "fucking", "cock", "pussy", and such within their work of literature.

X-*treme* titles differ from E-rated titles only in plot premise and storyline execution. Unlike E-rated titles, stories designated with the letter X tend to contain controversial subject matter not for the faint of heart.

Also by Ann Jacobs

ॐ

Print books:

A Mutual Favor

Black Gold: Another Love

Black Gold: Dallas Heat

Black Gold: Firestorm

Black Gold: Sandstorms

d'Argent Honor 2: Eternally His

Enchained

Lawyers in Love: The Defenders

Lawyers in Love: The Prosecutors

Mystic Visions *(anthology)*

E-Books:

A Mutual Favor

Another Love

Awakenings

Bittersweet Homecoming

Captured *(anthology)*

Colors of Love

Colors of Magic

Dallas Heat

Dark Side of the Moon

d'Argent Honor 1: Vampire Justice

d'Argent Honor 2: Eternally His

Enchained *(anthology)*

Firestorm

Forever Enslaved

About the Author

❧

Ann Jacobs is a sucker for lusty Alpha heroes and happy endings, which makes Ellora's Cave an ideal publisher for her work. Romantica™, to her, is the perfect combination of sex, sensuality, deep emotional involvement and lifelong commitment — the elusive fantasy women often dream about but seldom achieve.

First published in 1996, Jacobs has sold over forty books and novellas, more than a few of which have earned awards including the Passionate Plume (best novella, 2006), the Desert Rose (best hot and spicy romance, 2004) and More Than Magic (best erotic romance, 2004). She has been a double finalist in separate categories of the EPPIES and From the Heart RWA Chapter's contest. Three of her books have been translated and sold in several European countries.

A CPA and former hospital financial manager, Jacobs now writes full-time. She loves to hear from readers. You can find her website and email address on her author bio page at www.ellorascave.com.

D'ARGENT HONOR:
ETERNALLY HIS

ഔ

*D*edication

&

To my fabulous editor, SueEllen Gower, and my long-suffering critique partner, Joey Hill, who helped me bring the d'Argent vampires to life. I couldn't have done this series justice without your help.

*T*rademarks *A*cknowledgement

&

The author acknowledges the trademarked status and trademark owners of the following wordmarks mentioned in this work of fiction:

Band-Aid: Johnson & Johnson Corporation

Delta: Delta Air Lines, Inc.

Donna Karan: Gabrielle Studio, Inc.

Louis Vuitton: Louis Vuitton Malletier

Mercedes: DaimlerChrysler AG Corporation

Valentino: Valentino Couture, Inc.

Chapter One

ନ୍ଧ

"Where are you, you murdering bastard?"

Stefan curled his lips back in frustration, deliberately exposing his fangs. He wanted to take to the air, use his ability to race through time and space to confront his adversary, but he forced himself to wait. He stood, motionless in the shadows of a narrow alley within shouting distance of Atlanta's downtown business district. Straining his telepathic skills, he listened for a sound that should have had no relationship with death.

There it was. The soft, breathy moan of a woman in ecstasy.

He had him. Fourth floor of a decaying apartment hotel, a quarter-mile from where he stood.

Stefan made two steps and took off in flight, with a whoosh of air and dangerous intent that would have made a passerby spin about nervously to see what threat had so briefly put his survival instincts on alert.

Like a silent cat, Stefan set down on the rickety landing of a rusty fire escape, but the moans had morphed into muffled wails and heartbreaking pleas. He had no time for subterfuge. An eerie silence replaced the sounds of struggling inside.

Fuck.

Stefan took a step back then rammed his booted foot through the windowpane and lunged inside. Shards of shattered glass crunched underfoot, announcing his presence.

There he was. Louis Reynard, the vicious murderer Stefan had been sent to track down after others of his clan had failed. The killer vampire stood over the still frame of yet another victim. Blood dripped from his prominent fangs, and his hulking body still trembled with the sensual pleasure of having just fed.

His eyes glowed when he stared at Stefan, and he let out a roar of fury.

Stefan harbored no illusion that his own power exceeded that of his much older adversary. But when he looked down at Louis' twentieth victim, unflinching wrath bubbled in his soul. He'd wipe the scourge of Louis Reynard off the earth or be destroyed himself.

He lunged. Reynard sidestepped. Then, suddenly, he swung out, but Stefan ducked under the powerful punch. His opponent might have outmatched him in strength and experience. But he had speed and agility. They performed a macabre dance, advance and retreat. Dodging what would have been a knockout punch, Stefan butted his head into his opponent's midriff.

Louis staggered back, but the blow wasn't enough to take him down. Pressing his advantage, Stefan brought up a knee and rammed it into Reynard's crotch.

"Fuck you. Now you die." Reynard lunged again. Stefan stepped aside just in time to avoid his opponent's vicious swing. When Reynard stumbled, Stefan hooked a leg around his ankle and sent him sprawling, following him down and pinning him beneath his own body.

Reynard bucked, nearly dislodging Stefan. He shifted, laid a forearm over the bastard's throat. Pushed hard. Knelt and bore down with most of his weight on Reynard's belly. A weaker opponent would have passed out. Not Reynard. He fought like a madman, full of bloodlust, bucking and sputtering and clawing at Stefan's neck and face.

Alina had been right. He shouldn't have tried to take Reynard down alone. Stefan's strength was fading fast. He had to finish this now, before the killer regained the advantage. Shifting his weight, he freed one hand and reached in his jeans pocket for the stake.

He let go of Reynard's neck, reared back to get the leverage he needed. As Stefan lifted the sharpened piece of rowan wood to slam through Reynard's black heart, Reynard jerked up with a burst of superhuman strength and sank his fangs into Stefan's cheek. Stefan snarled, yanked his head back. Reynard grinned around a mouthful of Stefan's flesh.

The murdering bastard bit me. Nausea welled up in Stefan's throat at the sight of blood trickling from the corners of Reynard's mouth. His own blood. A stinging pain shot through his right cheek. His stomach heaved at the taste of salty, metallic blood that bore the fetid taste of saliva from the killer vampire's fangs. The tainted fluid gathered at the corner of Stefan's mouth, burning its way down his chin as if it were caustic lye, not the fluid that sustained his kind.

Reynard bucked, tossing Stefan off him now as though he weighed no more than a child. While Stefan clutched his cheek, trying to stanch the flow of blood, his prey rolled away, sprang to his feet and leapt to the windowsill. "You sanctimonious little prig," he spat. "You've failed. Like all your inept kinsmen who've tried before you."

Stefan lunged, stake in hand. He raised it, made satisfying contact with Reynard's flesh. His belly, not his heart. Reynard jerked the stake from his belly. He laughed, the sound one of consummate evil. Then he disappeared into the night without another sound.

For a moment Stefan stood there, dazed, his cheek rent open and throbbing with agonizing pain. His nostrils tingled at the strong smell of blood. Human blood as well as his own. Warm. Fresh. Copious amounts of blood. It brought back memories of centuries ago, when he'd last fed on a mortal and not from a crystal tumbler in an upscale vampire bar. Lifeblood steeped in the smells of death.

Those memories flooded Stefan's soul with shame. But he had no time now to wallow in guilt. He had to drag himself up, check the woman. See if she still lived. Get help if she did.

As soon as he looked down at her, he knew Louis had finished the grisly task before he'd barged in. Crystal-like blue eyes stared up at him, unseeing. Shining blonde hair fanned out from a pale face, its ends matted with the congealing blood that pooled around her head from the gash in her throat.

Next to her lay the murderer's calling card, a white rosebud, obscene in its very purity and innocence. Louis had laid this one across his victim's slack, still fingers. Placed it carefully, as if in tribute. As if in thanks for her gift of sustenance, in recognition of his own revenge. The trademark of a crazed murderer, an inhuman monster, as sure as the cut throat and the familiar marks Stefan felt certain he'd find.

He knelt, looking closely. There they were. Two neat puncture wounds, practically invisible in the carnage of the *coup de grace*. Marks the local coroner would most likely attribute to anything but the true cause of this woman's death.

This woman was beyond help. The one Louis had probably already targeted as his next victim was not.

After making certain not to leave evidence behind that might point to him, Stefan left the way he'd come. He stood a moment on the landing, clearing his mind. Focusing on the killer, he tried to zero in on his location. For once, he succeeded. Good. He'd failed to destroy Reynard, but apparently he'd injured him badly. Badly enough, at least, that Reynard had temporarily dropped the shield that made it so difficult for Stefan to track him telepathically.

Stefan hurled himself into the air, followed the killer's tracks. To his surprise, he found himself landing at the main entrance to Hartsfield International Airport.

A constant stream of travelers passed by him as he strained to follow his prey's movements. He thought he'd caught the trail, shoved his way down the A concourse, muttering words of apology when he collided with a burly man, and again when a woman stopped just short of his outstretched arms. There he was! No, it was a mere mortal whose misfortune it was to resemble a killer vampire.

Stefan backtracked and propelled himself along a nearly deserted moving walkway toward another concourse. Reynard was buying a ticket on a Delta flight. Concourse B, said the sign above the ticket kiosk. Heedless of passengers who stared as he sprinted up the escalator, Stefan visualized his prey, found him at Gate Twenty-One.

Finally. Stefan arrived in time to watch Reynard hand a boarding pass to the attendant, meekly stepping aside with his carry-on bag for the unusually thorough security check undoubtedly occasioned by his tardy arrival and unkempt appearance. For a moment Stefan thought the guard would refuse to let Reynard board, but the other vampire's powers of persuasion apparently kicked in when a supervisor who'd been called questioned him about the cuts and bruises on his face and hands. It didn't take long before the examiner shook his hand and waved Reynard onto the jetway. Stefan glanced at the screen behind the desk. The plane was bound for Chicago.

Non-stop, the Delta ticket agent assured him when he asked. At least there was only one place Reynard could be going on this flight. Stefan could make it to Chicago in less time than it would take the commercial jet. Vampires hardly needed airplanes—unless they were hurt or sick and had lost some of their powers.

"Final boarding call for Delta Flight 258 with service to Chicago's O'Hare Airport."

Stefan made a quick mental calculation. The flight Reynard was taking would arrive in Chicago in about two hours, give or take. Locking in telepathically on his enemy, Stefan observed him winding his way down the jetway, taking his place in the last available first-class seat. Looking for all the world like a mortal businessman but for cuts and bruises that were quickly fading, Louis strapped himself in, closed the shade and rested his head on one of the small white pillows supplied to him by a smiling attendant.

Though he no longer had Reynard in his sights once the plane had left the ground, Stefan felt fairly confident that the other vampire would remain on that Boeing 757 until it landed—and that he could propel himself to O'Hare Airport in

15

time to find and tail the killer the moment he stepped past the security checkpoint.

Hurrying outside the bustling terminal into the velvet cloak of night, Stefan launched himself into the sky, willing himself to move through time and space toward the killer's destination.

* * * * *

In Chicago after a trip that had taken longer than he'd expected, Stefan detoured into a restroom to clean off grime from factory smokestacks and rid his body of the stench of fertilizer that had wafted its way upward from newly planted fields. He would have liked to soar above the clouds, but heavy air traffic along the Atlanta to Chicago corridor had made that hazardous, so he'd contented himself with flying low. Too low to avoid the pollution from heavily populated land.

Damn. Why did humans have to hang mirrors all over every public restroom? Eyes stinging from the reflected light, Stefan averted his gaze, looked instead at the dingy floor tile as he made his way to the bank of lavatories and wet his hands. When he put a hand to his cheek, he found blood was still seeping from the bite. Though cold water washed away the caustic saliva that still ate at his flesh, he imagined he'd suffer for days from aftereffects of vampire venom. Now he believed the rumors—Reynard's venom contained not only poison but also strong anticoagulation properties.

Poison and prevention of healing. A strong combination of weapons indeed. Weapons that almost made Stefan believe the legends about Reynard clansmen having been invincible in fights with other vampires, even older and stronger ones. Venom—Stefan dabbed another drop of blood from the throbbing wound—a fit weapon for a clan renowned throughout vampire history for its evildoing.

Reynard wouldn't be invincible this time. The d'Argent hunters would end his long, miserable existence.

Not wanting to miss his prey, he left the restroom. Reynard's plane would be arriving soon. Quickly locating the Delta concourse, Stefan stationed himself against a wall near the door arriving passengers would pass through once they'd deplaned. For a while, he pretended to read a day-old copy of the *Chicago Tribune* that some traveler had left on the windowsill.

How much easier it would have been if mortal lawmen had managed to connect the killings and put the combined resources of Interpol, the CIA and other international law enforcement agencies on Reynard's trail sooner. But Reynard had provided the only early evidence of his involvement to Stefan's cousin Alina, who'd been laughingly rebuffed when she'd offered help from the hunters of her clan. Even when the law enforcement community had finally accepted that the killings were all the work of one crazed vampire, they hadn't been able to catch up with him. And they still weren't willing to accept help from vampires.

Stefan stifled an oath. Why couldn't people accept that they sometimes needed vampires' help? They'd passed along too many legends, tales of vampire evil, from generation to generation. Those stories had proliferated the sort of fear Stefan had observed during most of his life. Fear that had made mortals destroy his father more than four hundred years ago.

Though the CIA and Interpol were finally seeking a serial killer, they'd never catch Reynard without the help of other vampires to destroy him. Most mortals, however fierce, tended to cringe at the idea of stakings and beheadings—the only effective methods for ridding Earth of a vampire as powerful as the one Stefan now stalked.

If he got half a chance, he would put a stake through Reynard's evil heart without a second thought.

Impatient, Stefan paced the length of the space in front of the security station. Why wouldn't the damn passengers hurry and deplane? Dawn was breaking now, and he'd have loved to be crawling into bed, not standing in an airport fighting the crowds. His usual means of travel beat airplanes and airports all to hell.

From a glance at the board that listed arrivals, he determined the flight had landed. When the first passengers charged down the hallway, Stefan straightened, immediately alert. He scanned the sea of faces coming toward him in undulating waves.

There he was, strolling down the walkway, rolling a suitcase that apparently belonged to the elderly woman smiling up at him as though he were her savior. Reynard looked innocuous. Even kind. Apparently he'd cleaned up on the plane, changed into fresh clothes free of his victim's blood. The bruises Stefan had inflicted had already faded, although he imagined Reynard was still hurting from the stake Stefan had sunk into his belly.

If only Stefan could take Reynard by surprise... No, he couldn't. Not only would he be disobeying Alina's strict order not to confront Reynard alone except in the direst of emergencies, but he'd be laying himself open to get arrested, thereby leaving Reynard unguarded to perpetrate his next act of evil.

Why couldn't Reynard have looked like the monster he was? If he had, Stefan could have enlisted the aid of some guards from the airport security force. All he could do was follow, observe, keep Reynard under careful surveillance until he led Stefan to his next intended victim.

The hell he would. If his reinforcements arrived and an opportunity arose, Stefan would try again to destroy Reynard, but only if they could do so in secrecy. He didn't relish having to make difficult explanations to mortal cops.

Stefan raised the newspaper to shield his face from view and began to follow his prey, careful to stay a few yards back. His fingers itched to tighten about the other vampire's muscular neck now, overwhelm him, spill his lifeblood as surely as he had slaughtered those twenty women. Stefan's cheek throbbed, the wound a painful reminder of his failure to stop Louis in Atlanta.

Fishing a handkerchief from his pocket, he dabbed away fresh blood that had again begun trickling from the deep laceration.

His stomach roiled as though he'd given in to temptation and sampled some delectable tidbit of human nourishment. When he watched Reynard assist his fellow passenger with two bulky bags, he wanted to heave. How could one so evil look so benign?

Stefan eased his irritation by imagining Reynard staked out in the sun, a wooden stake piercing his heart. Knowing his enemy was so near, in striking range, yet having to wait when his heart told him to confront the bastard now, went against every instinct in Stefan's soul.

He glanced through the automatic doors that led outside, noting that dawn had already broken in a clear blue sky. Good. According to information Alina had gleaned from a friend in Interpol, Reynard could tolerate very little sunlight. Already Stefan imagined enough bright rays were finding their way through the fluffy white cloud cover to sear the bastard's rotten hide. Although Stefan functioned fairly well in natural light, he blinked when he stepped out from under the shade of the overhanging roof. While his pupils adjusted, the sun beat down on his injured cheek, exacerbating the pain.

Stefan welcomed the sharp stinging sensation, the dull ache that surrounded it. It served to remind him of his quest and of the danger Reynard posed, not only to beautiful blonde females the world over but also to the d'Argent hunters charged with finding and destroying the serial killer. Slipping on mirrored aviator glasses, Stefan watched his prey pass over some bills to a uniformed driver and crawl into a darkened limousine behind his elderly companion.

Hurriedly, Stefan hailed a cab. While annoyed at the necessity of moving about conventionally, he resigned himself. If he propelled himself through space, hovering over the limo during early morning rush hour, somebody would be bound to notice.

"Follow that limo." Stefan had heard that on late-night TV, knew it sounded clichéd, but damn, it fit the occasion now.

The cabbie looked back at him, muttered something Stefan couldn't understand.

"Quickly. Don't let it out of your sight." Stefan pulled out his wallet. "I'll make it worth your while."

"Yes, sir." While Stefan barely understood the words, the glint in the eye of the driver assured Stefan he'd made his request quite clear. With seeming disregard for the increasingly heavy traffic, the cabbie wove in and out among speeding cars and trucks on the Northwest Expressway, not letting the limousine get more than two car lengths ahead.

Once the limo turned off the crowded interstate it began to angle east toward Lake Shore Drive. Tenement houses gave way to modest homes, row houses that had seen better days, and to the east a district of restaurants and clubs that bustled even at this early hour. Finally, on the other side of Rush Street, lush trees and manicured lawns flanked stately brownstones and apartment hotels.

Chicago's Gold Coast. Apparently Reynard intended to plan his next killing in style. The large homes were probably old by Chicago standards, though they seemed barely weathered compared with Stefan's own castle or the venerable buildings of Paris' Marais district.

When the limo pulled up beneath the portico of The Marquisa, a small luxury hotel a block from Lake Michigan, he leaned forward, one hand on the door handle. He'd get Reynard now, as soon as he'd checked in and retired to his rooms.

The old woman stepped out, leaning on her cane, gripping the edge of the door to pull her bent body from the limo. At the same moment, the trunk lid opened and the limo driver got out. As though he had all day, the driver retrieved her luggage and brought it around to the curb.

Stefan cursed, thrust a generous reward in his cabbie's hand and surged out of the cab. He approached the limo with a degree of caution, scanning its interior and the immediate surroundings, but he knew even before he shouldered past the surprised driver what he'd find inside. Nothing.

Reynard had eluded them again. Stefan straightened, concentrated. Still nothing. He couldn't connect with the older vampire. It was as though the bastard had drawn a curtain over his mind and disappeared without a trace.

Stefan's cheek throbbed. His muscles ached. What hurt the worst was knowing he'd have to admit to Alina that he'd failed…that not only had another woman died but he'd let Reynard slip through his fingers.

He'd reconnoiter. No time now to rest, for when Stefan slept, he lost all ability to make telepathic contact with his prey — not that he'd ever been able to do it consistently with Reynard anyway. Taking out his cell phone, he got the number of the hotel where the old lady had disappeared, called and reserved a room.

Instinct told him Reynard hadn't gone far. Stefan would start his search again, wait for the killer to let down his guard. This time he'd stop the killings. Destroy his prey.

Stefan glanced at his watch. Time for him to call Alina. She'd be awake now, probably enjoying the thimbleful of A-negative she took with the same regularity as mortals drank their morning coffee. She wasn't fond of being wakened — though she always granted Stefan the special privilege of taking his calls anytime, day or night. Stefan felt for his cousin, whose tranquil reign of their clan had been spoiled by Reynard embarking on this worldwide killing spree. All because she'd spurned his proposal.

No one, least of all Alina, had realized the repercussions of that day would lead them here. "Stefan, where are you?" Alina's concerned voice and the fact she picked the phone up immediately underscored his importance to her, her confidence in him. It also sharpened the edge of his guilt.

"I lost him. I'm sorry, I knew you were counting on me. We'll find him. I won't let him give me the slip again. I swear it. I almost caught him, but — "

"You faced him alone?"

Stefan winced as his gentle cousin's voice snapped across the line with all the power of the queen of the d'Argent clan.

"If I'd gotten there a moment sooner, his victim would still be alive."

There was a long pause. "I told you this would not be an easy assignment," she said at last, sighing. "You sound tired, cousin. Come to me and we'll talk."

"Now? You want me to leave when I've got to be close on his trail?"

"I want you at your fighting best. You haven't fed, and I'm telling you to come home. If it makes you feel better, I will dispatch Claude to watch the area for Reynard while you care for your own basic needs."

Stefan gritted his teeth. "With all due respect, Alina, Claude should be allowed to enjoy at least a few more weeks with his bride. Not to mention that we don't want to risk him going up against this monster alone. After all, he's practically a child—no more than seventy-five years old. What if Reynard decides to accelerate his schedule? I have a feeling—"

"We haven't the luxury of allowing our uncle to luxuriate in the carnal pleasures that follow a new mating. Not until the Fox is destroyed." Alina paused for a long minute. "You believe Reynard will strike again in the next several days?"

"No. Probably not that soon. But I wouldn't be surprised if he kills again before the next full moon." The Fox. Though the nickname came from the English for Reynard, Stefan thought it apt. The vampire was as wily and elusive as his namesake of the forest.

"Then come and tell me about this. Take time to prepare. Don't make me order you as your queen." Her voice softened. "Come home because your cousin wants to see you."

Damn it, Stefan had never been able to deny Alina anything. Besides, she was right. He did need rest and sustenance—and whatever knowledge she had that she'd only convey to him in person. "I'll come as soon as Claude lets me know he's arrived."

Chapter Two

ဢ

No wonder Alina's rejection had sent Louis into a killing frenzy. Stefan adjusted his mirrored shades as he watched her emerge from *rue des Rosiers*. Six hundred years old and counting, his beautiful cousin looked every inch the ageless vampire queen.

Her sleek blonde hair caught the sun's rays, giving her an angelic appearance. As she approached, Stefan's gut clenched with fury, for he was reminded of those other women singled out because they'd looked enough like Alina to be her doubles. By the time Reynard had finished with them, they'd no longer had Alina's animated smile, her sensuous way of moving that made humans as well as males of their own species long to fall at her feet.

Like clockwork over the past year and a half, another victim had surfaced on the first night of each full moon, mute testimony to failure. Not only mortal law enforcers but also the finest hunters of the d'Argent clan had failed to stop the killer. Now Stefan, too, had arrived too late to prevent Reynard from murdering another innocent woman.

But he wouldn't fail again. He'd be back in Chicago within hours, unless Alina insisted he rest before making the return trip. Finally, they had Reynard more or less in their sights, and when he moved on his next victim, they'd be there to take him down. Save a woman's life where they'd been unable to do so before.

So Stefan wouldn't have the rest of his days haunted with memories of those who'd died. So Alina could quit blaming herself for something that wasn't her fault. After all, the d'Argents had fought evil vampires like the Reynards for centuries. Only a fool would have believed Louis Reynard had given up his murdering, thieving ways overnight and become the kind of vampire he'd pretended to be when he'd vied for Alina's favors.

Alina certainly was no fool. She'd had no intention of treating Reynard with more than the courtesy one clan ruler accorded another.

"You have no reason to blame yourself. No rational being would have considered that Reynard might have had the mistaken impression that if you became his mate, he'd suddenly regain the ability to copulate." Stefan shook his head. They'd known—everyone in the vampire world had known for centuries that only born vampires could mate like humans. He longed for the day his cousin's smile would once more reach her beautiful eyes. The day when Louis Reynard no longer lived to taunt her with his evil.

A gentle breeze played in a budding tree whose bright-green leaves shaded him from the noonday sun in the *Place des Vosges*. The sounds of life, of mortals going about the daily business of living made the discomfort at being outdoors on this sunny day worthwhile. The smells of coffee and freshly baked pastries stimulated him as though at some time in his long life he'd required mortal sustenance—which he had not, for like all the ruling family of the d'Argent clan, he was a vampire born.

He closed his eyes and felt Alina approach, tilting his head slightly to the left to feel the touch of the wind. For a moment he visualized his home, imagining clean country air wafting over his naked body while he lay in the same ornately carved bed where he'd been born four hundred and fifty years ago. His eyes would open to dim light muted by opulent draperies that swayed gently in front of tall, narrow windows. Stefan longed for the ancient castle set on the cliffs of Normandy—where he'd someday take a *dhampir* bride and, if the fates allowed, produce a son or daughter to carry on the d'Argent legacy. He wouldn't be going back there, though, until he succeeded in destroying Reynard.

Alina sat down across from him. "You look terrible. When are you going to learn to eat sensibly?" The concern of a friend, a mother and something more, something that connected them even beyond lovers, was in her tone. It renewed Stefan's resolve, made him put the longing away. The bond of years, of clinging together against a sometimes hostile mortal world, was too strong to break with ease. There wasn't anything he wouldn't do, or give up, for Alina or for their clan.

He opened his eyes and turned his head. Alina's eyes narrowed, and her hand shot out and touched the Band-Aid he'd used to cover his cheek. He jerked his head away when she tugged it off then made a deliberate effort to be still, allow her examination of the laceration that hadn't yet healed, evidence that the wound had been inflicted by another, more powerful vampire's fang.

"Reynard did this to you," she spat out.

Stefan had hoped she wouldn't look beneath the bandage. He didn't want to add to the worries that clouded her expression. "Close call." He caught her gently by the wrist, laid a kiss on her palm. "I left him with a few dents and dings too. Impaled his belly with a stake. I arrived in time to catch him but not in time to prevent the crime. Like Alex and Claude and the others, I was unable to destroy him. As I told you on the phone, the bastard yet lives. And I can't maintain telepathic contact with him." The admission hung bitter on his tongue.

A single tear slid from expressive eyes as true and distinct a green as he'd been told his own were. D'Argent eyes, his mother called them. Stefan hated to gaze into Alina's when they glistened with tears. He'd seen her troubled for too long, known she'd become desperate when she'd come to him last month and commanded that he take up the search himself, find Reynard and stop him in his bloody tracks. "It's not your fault, sweetheart."

"It is. I should be out searching for the fiend myself, destroying him once and for all. Not risking you and Alex and the others."

"Hush. The clan needs you. We'd not risk you. I will take care of Louis. You take care of us. How is Alexandre faring?" Stefan worried about their young cousin, whose reckless abandon had practically been his destruction six weeks earlier, when he and Claude had tracked Reynard to a vampire bar in Buenos Aires and tried to take him out between killings.

"He's healing nicely. Champing at the bit to get out of his bed and rejoin the hunt." She paused, took Stefan's hand. "I know I shouldn't worry. You're both grown-up males who can take care of yourselves. It's just...Reynard is so old, so strong. It would destroy me if—"

"He won't. We won't let him. Remember, we're vampires born. Our powers exceed that of any made vampire, no matter how long he's managed to survive."

Alina glanced toward the infamous *Place de la Concorde*, then met his gaze. "Cease your typical male posturing. When you boast, you sound like a little boy in the schoolyard. I agree we are strong. But we're not invincible. I remember watching the headman's axe come down on your papa's neck, knowing that when his head left his body, he was lost to us forever. I order you to take care."

Her words raised images in Stefan's mind, images that should have dulled after so many years, of the time when Catherine de Medici ruled as regent and the streets of the *Marais* district ran red with blood. His ears rang, bombarded with the echo of sounds he'd never forget—shouting vendors hawking their wares while jugglers distracted cheering onlookers from the carnage and the pickpockets on execution days. "Thankfully, civilization has moved past St. Bartholomew's Day and Catherine's madness."

Stefan shook off the grief that still tore at him over four hundred years after he'd lost his beloved father. His throat stung. His fangs ached. Weakness flowed through his veins. Damn, but he needed to feed soon, before hunger robbed him of all his strength. He glanced toward his favorite haunt, *Le Sang des Rosiers.* "May I buy you a glass of your favorite sustenance?" he asked, inclining his head toward the side street—and the bar.

Alina shot him a smile that almost made him forget his hunger. "When are you going to learn not to be so fastidious about where you feed? Alex tells me you disappointed yet another possible mate before you took up the chase for Louis, by refusing to take her offering of blood."

Like his mother and others of the clan, Alina worried about his reclusiveness. He suspected she'd called him from his self-imposed exile not only because she trusted him to destroy Reynard but because she also thought he needed to get away from his lonely castle. She was always pushing him to seek some feminine companionship. "You're as bad as my mother, sweetheart. You should know by now I'll not risk overindulging, turning another mortal woman's sexual high into her final moment on this earth."

Centuries had passed, yet the memory still haunted him of that day when he'd been a reckless youth and done just that—fed too enthusiastically and, rather than turning his lover into one like him, caused her death. The sight of Tina's lifeless body, so pale and helpless and still, haunted him yet today. "That's why when I mate, it will be with a *dhampir* at least, if not one of my own kind."

"Vampires born are hard to come by, my sweet cousin. Even *dhampirs* born of a vampire father and a mortal mother who's been turned are scarce enough. If only we were not of such close kin…" Alina's voice trailed off, as though she'd have liked for them to be more than beloved cousins.

Not so, Stefan knew, for they'd been more like sister and brother than cousins, loving and teasing each other for as long as he remembered. Alina had tended his childhood cuts and bruises, shared his darkest secrets, and helped extricate him from the consequences of his youthful exuberance. They knew each other too well ever to succeed as lovers.

"…and if only you weren't centuries too old for me." Deliberately, Stefan taunted her, not anxious to pursue the subject of his love life or lack thereof. "Come. Let's go inside out of this noonday sun. I'll catch you up on my search, tell you how I located Reynard and, regrettably, how he escaped my surveillance. Perhaps you can give me the advice of an elder as to how I may best destroy him before he kills again."

"If you don't stop harping on my age, this 'elder' will make sure you finish your days as a cruise-ship director in the Bahamas." Alina's quicksilver grin made Stefan's breath catch in his throat, just as their teasing each other with threats of horrifying tortures each knew would never be imposed reminded him of other, happier times. "You look as though you could use some shade and a nice, chilled drink. Shall we head to the bar?" Her voice was light, but her expression turned serious. Reynard's sinister shadow touched them even in this sun-dappled park.

"Need you ask?" He took her hand and steered her toward the narrow, tree-shaded street.

As they sat at a small round table in the back of the bar in the *rue des Rosiers*, Stefan fed thoughtfully from a stemmed crystal glass, savoring the salty, metallic fluid that sustained him. Alina urged him to order a second glass while she sipped daintily on the aperitif she'd had the barman lace with half a thimble full of anisette.

"Relax, cousin. I know you don't believe Claude's experienced enough to deal with Reynard should it become necessary, but he certainly can be trusted to stake out the area where you last saw Reynard, in case he should return. Alex says he acquitted himself very well in Buenos Aires."

Stefan shook his head. "I know. But I'd rather be there myself. We can't let Reynard kill again." The old ones of their clan—his mother included—had begun to fret. They worried that this string of killings by an evil vampire would become widely known to mortals and set off another vampire hunt like ones that had thinned their numbers in centuries past. Hunts that had lost them powerful elders like his father and Alina's, either of whom could have taken on Reynard and defeated him, one on one.

As a result, the d'Argent clan Alina led was young by vampire standards. They needed experience, fast. Claude was a prime example. Stefan was fond of his young uncle and in less serious circumstances wouldn't have worried that Claude might be destroyed in a confrontation with most enemies. But then Reynard was not most enemies. It would take more than one of them — no matter how skilled a fighter — to bring down the Fox.

Alina shot a disgusted look at the laceration on Stefan's cheek. "Males. Every one of you suffers delusions that you're indestructible. I told you when I asked you to join the hunt — against my better judgment, mind you, for I hate to risk losing you and having to tell your mother she's lost another loved one — not to take undue risks. It would destroy your mother to lose you too. Reynard has a few hundred years on you, and you'd do well to remember it."

"I know." The last thing Stefan wanted was to cause his mother more pain. "Surely there's a way to counter his advantage."

"Go at him very carefully. And I order you not to go alone. Forget your foolish notions of chivalry and fair play. Use Claude. Alexandre too, for he's recovering quickly and I fear we'll not be able to keep him down much longer." Alina paused, her expression serious but full of obvious distaste for Reynard. "Among the three of you, I'm sure you'll be able to find a way to destroy Reynard."

Stefan nodded his agreement, although it rankled to admit he didn't have the strength to take care of Reynard alone. As he drained his glass, though, he realized Alina was right. Getting rid of the serial killer was more important than pandering to his own ego. "The more I think of it, the surer I am that he's about to change his pattern of killing on the first night of the full moon."

Setting her glass down, Alina looked at Stefan, her expression troubled. "You mentioned him not appearing near the murder scene until a few days before he strikes. What makes you believe he's in Chicago now to stalk his next victim?"

"The rose. The past three kills, he's marked seven days before the full moon with a white rose on the doorstep of his victims. And the notes he's sent you. The first few arrived after the killings and merely named the city, but now they're — "

"I know. The notes are now arriving days in advance, naming the victims. I received this one just as I was leaving to meet you. It gives not only the next victim's name but her address as well."

"Give it to me."

"Here." Alina pulled out an envelope, the kind mortals used for formal invitations, and handed it to Stefan. "Don't fly off until we've finished this discussion, no matter how much you'll want to. As soon as I read the message, I contacted Claude and ordered him to take a hotel room overlooking this house. He contacted me as we were walking to the bar to assure me that Louis hasn't shown his face."

His hand not quite steady, Stefan slid the heavy vellum sheet from the envelope, opened the single fold, and focused on the three lines written in ornate script in reddish-brown ink — no, blood. Vampire blood. *Julie Quill. Twenty-eight Delaney Street, Chicago.*

He clenched his fists, tried to curb his rage at the macabre invitation to a killing yet to take place. A challenge by Reynard, a boast that nothing his pursuers could do would stop him. A claim that he was invincible.

Stefan managed to stifle a few choice words unfit for his royal cousin's ears. "Think, Alina. For over a year Reynard maintained identical patterns. A note, naming a city, sent from that city the day of the killings there, the first day of each full moon. A victim, eerily similar in appearance to you. Then, subtle changes in the notes. The roses left on the victims' steps seven days before the murders, as well as the ones left with the bodies. I say he's going to alter the pattern of his killings even more. Kill at times other than on the full moon."

Alina leaned forward, clasped both of Stefan's hands. "I'm afraid you may be right."

"I'll keep Claude watching Ms. Quill while I find and stake out Reynard." Stake. That was the operative word. If he had his way, Stefan would destroy the killer vampire before he struck again. He'd relish sinking every centimeter of his sharp-pointed rowan stake into Reynard's evil heart. Chopping the head off his lifeless body. Watching the sun turn it into nothing but a pile of dust.

"No," Alina said, her tone commanding. "We can do no less than protect this woman with the best we have. That's you. Go to Julie. Do whatever you must to gain her trust. Be with her every moment of the day and night. Use the vampire persuasion for which you're so well known. Seduce her. Employ force if you must, but don't let her out of your sight. Let Claude keep an eye out for Louis. Meanwhile, I will get a team set up so, by the time the moon waxes again, you can communicate with them all when Louis makes his move. Until then, it will have to be you and Julie together."

Stefan clenched his fists. How like Reynard to taunt them, boast of his ability to take out victims right under their noses. "I don't like it, but I suppose Reynard has reason to believe he can outsmart us all. Are you sure you trust me to watch over this woman he's marked as his next victim?"

"There's no one I trust more. With your history, you should be able to remain focused and disciplined, even around a beautiful mortal who's under your seductive powers." Alina smiled, but from the glint in her eyes, Stefan imagined she was mentally playing matchmaker. He could practically hear her brain grinding away, wondering if putting him in proximity with Reynard's next intended victim would awaken his passion, cure the emotional darkness he'd embraced for nearly two centuries.

By this time Alina should have learned. Accepted his decision to remain emotionally aloof, to resist temptation until such time as he chose to single out a female of his clan and claim her. But no. Alina was a hopeless romantic, certain there was a mortal woman who'd steal his heart, make him willing to risk all to claim her. "I'll do what you say, but you're wrong. This woman can be no more to me than an assignment. Hopefully a very pleasant one.

"Speaking of pleasurable assignments, cousin, who do you have watching over you? You do realize, do you not, that Reynard imagines his final victim will be you."

Alina smiled. "Your mother and mine have set a full dozen d'Argent vampires to guarding me. Would you like for me to call them out of hiding, reassure you I take no unnecessary risks?"

"That won't be necessary. I trust you. It's probably for the best that they don't show themselves, for if Reynard should attack you, they can take him from behind." Stefan hated the need for subterfuge, the knowledge that he lacked the power to confront this enemy directly and succeed. "Shall we go now and visit Alexandre?"

"Yes. He's recovering quickly now, and I'm certain he'll insist on joining you and Claude in Chicago long before the next full moon."

*   *   *   *   *

Late the next afternoon, Stefan spotted a small, elegant bar across the street from Chicago's Lincoln Park, not more than a block from where Julie Quill lived. After his long journey, he needed the darkness, sought the cool, welcoming atmosphere inside. He stepped through the dark wooden door, the tools of his trade neatly ensconced in a black leather satchel he'd bought this morning at Louis Vuitton's Paris showroom.

Though he'd fed yesterday, his mouth watered at the thought of sipping something cool, wet, rare. A spritzer of AB-negative, made with sparkling water from one of France's finer springs. Pity this wasn't a vampire bar. More was the pity that he hadn't located one yet among the clubs and eateries in this upscale neighborhood or along Rush Street. He'd taken Alina's warning to heart. He'd feed more consistently, wherever vampire sustenance was available. He had to keep up his strength, and he couldn't afford to be choosy.

He sat at a table in the front, close to a plate-glass window overlooking Lincoln Park, watching the mortals pass by and inhaling the aroma of steaming sausages, hard-boiled eggs, the pungent aroma of dark beer on tap. Consciously, he smiled, being careful not to show his fangs. Blending in with the other customers who apparently made this their after-work watering hole didn't seem too difficult.

In front of him, a couple sat close together on the same side of the tufted, red leather booth, their sides touching, the man's arm cradling the woman's shoulders. As though he'd come straight from work to meet his girlfriend, the man wore a gray pinstriped business suit. She wrapped her fingers around the burgundy-striped tie he had on, caressing his skin beneath the placket of the second and third buttons of his starched white shirt.

Stefan's cock stirred as he watched the man slide his hand down the back of his girlfriend's short T-shirt and caress the line of skin above the waistband of her low-riding jeans—blatant sexual foreplay. It had been too damn long since he'd taken a lover. Too long since he'd enjoyed a woman's touch, her kiss, the heat of her body warming his cool, dry skin.

For a moment he closed his eyes, imagined the tight wet heat of a lover's cunt around his cock, squeezing...soft hands cupping his sac, rolling his balls in a rhythmic motion that coaxed out his seed...the even tighter asshole gripping him when he fucked her there, and the taste of her blood on his fangs when he nipped her plump, round buttocks. His mouth watered when he opened his eyes, saw the man fingering his girlfriend's prominent nipples through her thin T-shirt. Desire slammed through him, made his cock press painfully against the zipper of his slacks.

Stefan needed a woman. Needed to fuck away the pain of long-unsatisfied desire.

No. Sex drained his energies. He needed to focus now on destroying Reynard...protecting the killer's next intended victim. Come to think of it, though, part of his assignment could easily involve appeasing his long ignored sexual appetite. On one plane, that disturbed him. On another, the idea had his slow heartbeat accelerating, pumping blood, anticipating...

"What'll you have, handsome?" A buxom, dark-haired waitress smiled down at him.

Stefan hesitated. "A draft, please." He couldn't drink it, but the aroma of dark imported beer would tickle his nostrils while keeping him from drawing undue attention from the other patrons in the bar.

"Comin' right up. Can I get you some peanuts? A sausage?"

"No, thank you." It was damn inconvenient having to pretend he was a human. "Perhaps later." He coughed, covering his mouth with one hand. Wouldn't do for the waitress to notice his fangs, though he'd found few people actually took that close a look—or if they did look, they apparently didn't place any significance on the fact his incisors were longer and more pointed than he'd ever observed on anybody outside the vampire clans.

For a long time Stefan nursed the dark, rich brew, occasionally lifting the frosted mug and wetting his lips. The taste of hops and wheat was pleasant on his tongue, but he dared not swallow. Even now, after all this time, the memory of having imbibed a mortal's drink of choice once when he'd been young and foolish—or rather, of having suffered through the aftereffects of having done so—remained vivid in his mind. A day spent tossing in his bed, doubled up from the pain in his gut, retching for hours until all the stuff came up, was an experience he had no intention of repeating.

He set down the mug and glanced at the scene on the street outside. Dusk made the light green leaves of towering elm trees glisten against a darkening sky. He liked the mysterious, sensual look of the tree-lined boulevard just as night was falling, the dim street lamps glowing in the deepening dusk.

As his attention lingered on the peaceful tableau, a frisky dachshund came into view, checking out the messages left on every tree and bush, as was the nature of a dog. Stefan enjoyed watching the canine, observing its simple joy in the act of being walked. His gaze rose the length of the bright-blue leash to the dog's owner.

He sensed that he'd just found Reynard's next victim, and if he'd imagined he could seduce her and stay detached emotionally, he was most likely wrong. Like Alina, this woman was blonde and beautiful. She even had a similar, brilliant smile and a way of walking that conveyed self-confidence. From her carriage, her smile and the ladylike swing to her walk, Stefan concluded that she knew she attracted male attention and liked the knowledge that she did. His cock twitched in silent salute.

He spotted Claude, following the woman at a safely discreet distance. Yes, this was Julie Quill. Concentrating, he made contact with his associate. "I'm here now, Claude. Go on back to the hotel and stay on the lookout for Reynard."

The couple in the booth next to him rose, apparently deciding it was time to take their lovemaking to a more private setting. The woman handled the tip by putting her hand in the man's pants pocket to draw out some folded money, obviously giving him an intimate caress in the process. Discomfited at the blatant loveplay, Stefan glanced away, shifting his gaze back to the window.

He bolted up straight in his seat, his testicles tightening in cold dread. There stood Reynard, next to the woman on the sidewalk. The bastard looked like thousands of others who walked along the shady boulevard bordering the park. Reynard bent to pet the dog, laughing as though he thought it funny that the small creature's hackles rose and she bared her small, sharp teeth.

At least the dog knew when it had met a foe.

In the short time he'd been part of the hunt, Stefan had seen this in his mind a hundred times—Reynard's smiles, his courtly manner, his slow enticement of his victim until the next full moon, when he'd taken her, promised ecstasy and delivered death instead. Now he was witnessing the killer's seduction dance in real time—the meeting, contrived to look accidental.

He tuned in on the casual conversation.

"May I see you home?"

There it was, the first step, an offhand invitation delivered in a genteel, deep voice tinged with the slightest hint of a European accent. Damn, Louis's pitch wasn't all that different from conversations Stefan himself had struck up with countless beautiful women over the centuries. His stomach muscles clenched. He'd never killed a lover by design. Never killed at all but once, when he'd been young and reckless, carried away by bloodlust.

Though he and Alina had agreed he wouldn't let the killer know of his presence, something compelled Stefan to get closer. Move within striking range in case Reynard decided to amend his schedule. Stefan rose, laid some bills on the table, and stepped outside, unable to fight down the certainty that, predictable as the killer had been over the past twenty months, this time he'd alter his pattern. Stefan crept closer, staying in the shadows of the trees, listening. Delving into his prey's mind, hoping Reynard wouldn't sense an adversary's presence and draw down the curtain on his private thoughts.

Belle Jolie, I cannot wait…dine on your luscious flesh…end of the full moon's waning.

Stefan imagined Reynard's incisors lengthening, as though in readiness for the appearance of that slender crescent in a midnight sky.

Reynard's words erased any doubt in Stefan's mind that this was Julie. And if Stefan read Reynard correctly, the killer planned to strike again in no more than a few short days.

Stefan's instincts hadn't been too far off. His muscles quivered with the need to act, but he held back, concentrating on his prey, wanting to catch all the nuances of thought in the other vampire's twisted mind.

Staying far enough back to avoid detection, he watched and listened, but it was as though Reynard had deliberately blocked off his innermost thoughts. He spoke to Julie of his travels, the weather, the fact his favorite flower was the rose—the white rose. Stefan's gut twisted, but Julie obviously caught nothing sinister in that admission, for she remarked that she liked white roses too.

Stefan sensed Julie's innate kindness, her enjoyment of people and her surroundings. Her smile was open, trusting. Too trusting. Her thoughts seemed as open as Reynard's were closed.

Reynard was wooing her with vampiric compulsion. Stealing away the wariness of strangers that she'd have learned at her mother's knee. Stefan had to clamp down on his own impulsive need to take the killer down right now.

Apparently Reynard's only emotion was rage, his only motivation revenge and retribution. Though he strained his mind, Stefan intercepted nothing soft in his prey's feelings. Reynard apparently didn't even harbor overtly lustful thoughts—and if any woman could raise a made vampire's lust, it was this one. She certainly raised his own libido more than a notch or two.

Stefan dared not wait to make his move until Alex rejoined them. He had to do something to thwart the killer now, before it was too late. Hanging back, out of sight, he followed Reynard and Julie to the pristine brownstone at 28 Delaney Street, in plain sight of the hotel where the old woman who'd accompanied Reynard from the airport had checked in earlier.

Where Claude was keeping a watchful eye on Julie's house and watching for Reynard's return.

No doubt Claude had stationed himself in the hotel lobby once he realized Stefan had taken over surveillance of Julie. Stefan imagined his associate would be diligently scanning the faces of all who entered or departed, hoping to spot Reynard. Stefan shook his head. If he knew his very young uncle — and he did — he'd find Claude growing impatient, venturing outside. By now he'd be baking in the late afternoon sun in order to be in better position to spot their prey.

Stefan couldn't influence Reynard's thoughts, so he zeroed in on Julie's mind. He had to reach her, compel her to obey his desperate plea. *Don't let him in. He means you harm.*

That little dog of Julie's faced off against Reynard, her short legs planted firmly on the concrete stoop, hackles raised and teeth bared.

"Noodles, no." Julie bent, lifting the dog just as she prepared to sink her fangs into the fine wool of Reynard's gray slacks. "I don't know what's gotten into her. She usually exhibits better manners with people she meets."

Julie. Listen to Noodles. Don't let this stranger into your home.

When she glanced around, as though looking for the source of the voice in her head, Stefan realized he'd connected with Julie. She'd heard him and was considering what he'd said. Not wanting to alert Reynard as to his presence, Stefan stayed hidden behind a spruce hedge across the street, and the shadows of approaching darkness further obscured him from their view.

Never before had he connected so quickly with a mortal. Stefan took this as a sign — a sign that if he seduced this woman, he himself would be hard-pressed to hold on to his own emotions. He must, though, for if he let her seduce him, he'd suffer incredible pain when he had to leave. While she'd have only a vague recollection of their liaison, his own memories would remain crystal clear for all eternity.

Julie smiled, murmured a goodnight to Reynard, and went inside with her astute pup. Waiting, his body tense, prepared for trouble should the other vampire force the issue, Stefan watched the killer vampire stare at her closed, dark-blue door.

Reynard turned slowly on his heel, fixed his gaze directly on Stefan's hiding place—and dipped his head. A flash of arrogant fang, and then he was gone as though he'd never been there at all.

Fuck. There was no time to lose. Stefan stepped out of the bushes. It was time for him to make his move and become Julie's bodyguard, up close and personal.

Chapter Three

ॐ

"Well, we met a new friend, Noodles. You didn't act as if you liked him very well." Julie Quill bent, unsnapped the dog's leash and scratched her sleek, smooth back. "What's the matter, girl, did you smell some mean old cat on the man's slacks?"

Noodles growled and her hackles rose. Funny, how such soft fur could turn so stiff, so fast. Julie shrugged. No telling what had made Noodles take an instant dislike to Mr. Reynard. The dog generally adored attention. She loved everybody, even strangers who stopped to pet her in the park.

Louis Reynard. The name sounded French, but Julie hadn't been able to place the accent. The man himself had a compelling way about him, generated a level of sensual awareness Julie hadn't experienced for a long time. Too long. Though he wasn't what she'd call handsome, he had a face she wouldn't soon forget. An interesting face. Well-cut, dark brown hair, just a bit overgrown, went well with his flashing dark eyes, a prominent nose that looked as though it might have suffered a couple of fractures over the years, and a sensual mouth she guessed seldom broke into a full-fledged grin. Mr. Reynard's face would translate well onto canvas. He could have been thirty-five or fifty. Julie hadn't been able to peg him the way she could most people she met. An investor, he'd said—but he hadn't said what he invested in.

The man had fascinated her, so much she'd broken her rule about steering clear of strangers and come within words of inviting him inside. Until a voice—a strong voice in her head— had warned her to take care. It was almost as if that voice had come from outside her being…a male voice, deep and compelling, a voice she hadn't been able to ignore. Maybe…

Noodles barked.

"Sorry, girl, I almost forgot to give you your supper." She poured some kibbles into the dog's bowl and refilled her water tank, then sat at the kitchen table and looked out the window at a brilliant sunset.

Julie's mind kept returning to the man she'd met. There was something about him — something that compelled her to see him again. Maybe she would take Louis Reynard up on his invitation for drinks and dancing tomorrow night.

* * * * *

Stefan moved stealthily through the night, checking the security of Julie's townhouse, intercepting her thoughts occasionally when he glimpsed her through glass panels in the sturdy patio door. When she debated with herself as to whether to meet Reynard again, he suppressed the urge to break in, persuade her of her foolishness, make her believe the bastard had designs on her life.

You'll see that murderer again over my dead body.

The only vampire Julie might be dancing with any time soon would be him. Stefan stepped back from the door. In the morning he'd contrive to meet Julie. For now, he sensed she was safe from the Fox, for he didn't feel Reynard's evil presence. Still he stayed, lurking in the shadows, offering the protection of his body against any who might threaten her.

He'd begin the seduction that had become more than a duty the moment he'd seen her face, heard her voice, watched the loving way she handled her frisky pup. He'd stroke the satiny skin of her cheek, her slender throat, taste the sweetness of her full, sensuous mouth. As mortal females inevitably did to born vampires, she'd respond to whatever irresistible force it was that he possessed. She wouldn't understand the compulsion that would drive her to him, but that wouldn't matter. Forgetting propriety, abandoning caution, she'd tangle her tongue with his...curl her long, slender fingers around his rock-hard cock...bare her throat with its tempting throbbing vein and beg him to take her.

He'd answer her demands. Fuck her cunt and ass and mouth until she cried out her pleasure. Gorge himself on the feel of her body against his own, warming him, driving him to come...to fill her with his seed as he sank his fangs into her pale, warm skin and drank his fill. No! He dared not give her a vampire kiss, must not allow himself the ultimate fulfillment he'd stood firm against for centuries.

Somehow he'd manage to control his carnal urges, as he'd done during his occasional sexual encounters with humans since inadvertently destroying Tina with his bloodlust. He'd seduce Julie, all right. He'd do it without stealing her mortality. Stefan's jaw tightened painfully, and his fangs ached. No. He'd deny them both the ultimate satisfaction. He wouldn't give in, no matter how she might beg. He clenched his fists, clamped down on his lust. She'd beg him to turn her. Take her out of the light and into his shadow world. Somehow he'd resist. He had to.

Stefan's body quickened as he anticipated the inevitable meeting. Despite his fears, he looked forward to being near her 24/7, as the American TV commentators often said.

Focus, d'Argent. Your job is to protect her.

That meant Stefan needed to rest before he approached her. Concentrating, he found Claude outside the hotel, scanning each face that passed by. "I need for you to watch our would-be victim for a while. Reynard's made contact with her."

"Already?" Claude lifted his sunglasses, rubbed at his eyes.

"Yes. If the Fox shows up anywhere, it will be there. At her townhouse. I must get some sleep, but I'll be along in a few hours to spell you."

Claude looked confused. "You saw him?"

"Yes, but he's not there now. He contrived to meet her at twilight, while she was walking her dog in Lincoln Park. After we switched off and I began to follow her."

"You want me to contact you if he shows up?"

"Yes. Under no circumstances are you to confront him by yourself." Stefan had no desire to have to inform Alina of the demise of their beloved young uncle. It would be just like the young, eager vampire to try to destroy Louis on his own—and lose. "You take care of yourself, for Marisa as well as your mother. I'll be upstairs," he said, not wanting to come off as maudlin or sentimental but figuring the best chance of having Claude take care involved reminding him of his responsibility to his brand new bride.

Surely Claude could handle this short surveillance without putting himself at risk. With luck, Alexandre would arrive within the next couple of days. When he did, Stefan would rest a lot easier.

Briefly he considered going to the police. *Right. As if they'd believe you if you did.* Few cops of his acquaintance admitted beings like him existed. The few who did, didn't welcome advice from vampires or believe some vampires had the good of mankind at heart. Damn, but he hated having humans look at him and see a creature to be feared and reviled.

His blood surged with fury. Fury that had fired his lifelong quest to hunt down and destroy bastards like Reynard. With every act of violence throughout the ages, rogue vampires had provided mortals good reason to fear them—and caused humans to fear all vampires, even the good ones like him and other members of his clan.

Stefan hated every evil vampire who walked the earth. No surprise. This recent spree of killings gave him ample reason to want Reynard destroyed. That was business. His business as a vampire hunter. Stefan didn't deceive himself, however. More drove him than duty or even disgust for the other vampire's heinous crimes. Vengeance not for what Reynard had recently done to twenty women, as much as for all the evil his kind had caused to thousands, more than four hundred years ago. Evil that had indirectly provoked a vampire hunt that had resulted in his father's destruction.

The sight of his father kneeling before the headsman, of blood running like water down the streets of Paris, had been burned into Stefan's soul when he'd been but a child. All the centuries-old wrongs mingled in Stefan's head with his current dilemma—how to thwart Reynard, protect Julie from his murderous intent.

He and his vampire team had to destroy the killer before he could strike again, and they damn well couldn't count on any help from human law enforcement.

Stefan stretched out on the bed, stifling a groan at the bliss of lying down for the first time in days. He felt something underneath his head, and he sought and found the chocolate a housekeeper had left on his pillow when she'd turned back the covers. He held it in his fingers a moment, turning the square from side to side, appreciating the gesture if not the substance of the small courtesy.

For centuries, he'd seen good and evil vie for supremacy in a variety of hearts, mortal as well as vampire. He'd realized the complicated play of the two in every mind. Every once in a while he'd encountered a soul whose light was so strong, there was little hope evil could take root.

Julie was just such a bright creature, an ironic counterpoint to his own darkness. His resolve hardened as he remembered her smile, her kindness to a stranger, the openness of her mind that had let her listen to the warning of her little dog...and of another stranger. If it took his last quivering burst of life, he'd stop Reynard from killing her.

He clenched his teeth, cursing when the tips of his fangs pierced his lower lip. He licked away two tiny droplets of his own blood. It tasted salty, rich, unlike the tainted flavor of the blood rent from his cheek by Reynard's venomous fang. His hand went up, fingered the bandage that had started his cheek to itching.

Something compelled him to get up, go to the window. With no difficulty, he picked Julie's house among the row of brownstones cast in eerie light by white lights spaced evenly along both sides of the street. He couldn't help it. Stefan couldn't say why, but he felt a gut-deep attraction to her that he hadn't experienced for years.

Perhaps he'd tell Julie about the danger she faced, once she came to trust him. He might even enlist her help in persuading the police to lend assistance—arrest Reynard for the grisly murder he'd committed in Atlanta. No, no prison built by mortals could hold a vampire of Reynard's age and experience. Not to mention that revealing his true nature right away would surely put a quick end to his plan to seduce Julie, win her trust.

He'd have to keep reminding himself that saving Julie's life was more important than satiating his lust. More important, even, than it would be to satisfy her compulsion to be totally consumed. An obsession all mortal females experienced under the seduction of a born vampire. He'd have to rein in every inbred impulse, satisfy the desire he'd build in her with conventional sex. Under no circumstance could he surrender, no matter how she pleaded. He dared not bestow a vampire kiss.

He wouldn't let Julie die. Too many women had already paid with their lives for Reynard's madness.

After peeling off the bandage that had been itching his face, Stefan toed off his loafers and stripped out of the wrinkled jeans and sweater he'd been traveling in for the better part of two days. With a sigh of exhaustion, he stretched out again on the king-size bed. A gorgeous blonde, endangered mortal invaded his mind...his cock. "Julie." Her name rolled easily off his tongue. Idly, he stroked his rapidly hardening flesh. Blood surged from his brain, flooding his lower body, leaving him lightheaded. No woman, vampire or mortal, had ever affected him quite this way.

Julie. A sunny name. A woman born in light, her golden skin kissed by his enemy, the sun. Stefan's balls tightened in their sac. Heat infiltrated his skin, headier than the flush he always experienced from feeding. He recognized it, welcomed it. It had been too long since he'd let passion overtake him. Too long since thoughts of any particular woman—a mortal, yet—

had invaded his being, made him want her so desperately he'd spill his precious, scarce seed on the sheets of a sterile hotel room bed, just to find release.

Eyes tightly closed though the room was dark, he wrapped his fingers harder around his rigid, pulsating cock, imagined Julie's softer touch there.

Her mouth was warm and wet on his throbbing flesh. Silken strands of her hair tickled his thighs. As she licked and sucked him, her fast, shallow breathing played an accelerating, rhythmic pattern along the ever hardening flesh of his cock. Oh, yes. Her hands warmed his testicles, caressing him there, coaxing out his essence.

He wanted to come. Wanted to give her his seed, watch her nurture it. See her bring forth another generation of d'Argent vampires. She'd ensure their immortality for yet another generation.

But not if he spilled his seed in her mouth. Groaning at the sudden coolness when he lifted her, regretting her little moan when she gave up his cock, he dragged her warm, satiny body along his. "Ride me, Julie."

Greedily she took him, surrounded him with her heat and moisture. Slowly at first, then faster, he lifted her, coaxed her to impale herself again. His sac drew up. His fangs elongated, anticipating...

The pressure built, starting in the pit of his stomach. Stefan's thigh muscles clenched. His testicles tightened as painfully as if caught in an unforgiving vise. His body strained, bent on gaining release denied it for much too long. His cock swelled against his own fingers, eager to spurt out his seed.

No! Coming now would drain his strength, and he needed it all for the confrontation with Louis. Besides, no matter how much she attracted him, Julie was mortal—and he'd sworn in centuries past never again to risk a mortal with his raging lust.

He'd make her want him, even take her to save her from Louis, but he wouldn't—mustn't—lose control and taste her blood. Turn her into one like himself—or destroy her as he'd destroyed Tina. Trembling, Stefan climbed out of bed and stepped under an ice-cold shower spray. It hadn't the desired effect, for although his skin prickled and his teeth chattered, his cock stayed rock-hard.

Painfully hard. This was not the time to let his sexual urges run wild. Stefan forced himself to plan, to plot Reynard's downfall, to recall his long-ago promise never to risk destroying another human female. Finally, his mind reclaimed control of his body and set him free from the arousal he dared not satisfy now. Free to sleep, a surprisingly refreshing sleep filled with dreams of a mate.

When he woke, Stefan stepped to the window again. It was still dark, but only a few hours before morning, he judged from the position of the moon in the black night sky. A few people hurried along the sidewalk, apparently heading to early appointments…or late-night assignations. His gaze settled on a flashy-looking brunette who'd just left the hotel and was teetering toward the cab stand on the corner in her skin-tight miniskirt and stiletto heels.

A prostitute. In Paris, Hong Kong or Chicago, they all had the same hardened, brittle look. The same world-weary expression. This one stopped to talk with a man in a dark suit, then hooked her arm through his elbow and let him lead her into a Mercedes limousine idling at the curb.

As the limo pulled away, Stefan saw his opportunity arise. Julie's front door inched open. Noodles trotted outside, her mistress tagging behind, apparently on a late-night walk for her to take care of business before curling up in her dog bed. Damn. The woman had no sense, venturing out this time of night with no protection but her dog. Quickly, he dressed and headed downstairs, determined to begin the job of seducing Julie—her mind as well as her luscious body.

* * * * *

What a beautiful night! A bright golden moon rose over Lake Michigan, and a light breeze ruffled Julie's hair as she walked along, Noodles in tow. Though she disliked going out alone so late at night, the dog had insisted, scratching and whining until Julie had grabbed her leash and given in.

She'd stay close to civilization, on the adjacent street where hotel doormen stood vigil all hours of the day and night. Meanwhile, she'd enjoy the cool air, the streetlights dotting the night with cheerful color.

When she glanced toward the hotel where her new friend Louis had mentioned he was staying, she saw him.

The most beautiful man she'd ever had the privilege of looking at up close. Tall, dark, with wavy black hair and…she knew even when looking at him fully clothed that he'd have a body she'd love to paint—or sculpt. His shoulder muscles rippled visibly beneath the v-neck sweater that clung lovingly to well-developed pecs and skimmed a flat belly she imagined would be deliciously ridged. Snug jeans outlined buns to die for, and an impressive bulge that made her itch to fondle his sex.

His features were half-hidden in the shadows, but even then she noticed a deep laceration on one cheek that gave him a rough-edged, dangerous look. A look that drew her, made her want to learn what secrets lurked behind an enigmatic smile. Though it was fully dark and she couldn't tell their color, she imagined his eyes would be a deep, rich brown, like the darkest, most succulent Belgian chocolate.

Julie had always been a sucker for Belgian chocolate. Pity she had to finish restoring the painting she'd promised by tomorrow for a restaurateur over on Oak Street. Even more was the pity her mama had raised her better than to accost a stranger on the street and proposition him then and there, because the temptation to do that nearly overwhelmed her.

What was she thinking? She'd never felt this way before about a man she hadn't even met. About any man. She couldn't drag her gaze off him, couldn't shake the feelings that had gripped her. A feeling that she'd come face to face with destiny.

Damn, but she wanted to paint him…taste him. She longed to stroke the classic planes of his face, explore all the textures in his short, professionally layered hair. Soothe that wound that marred his cheek and caress his chiseled jaw. Maybe…no, she'd felt desire, but nothing quite this intense before. No perfect stranger had ever before made her want to toss away good sense, throw herself into his arms.

When Noodles lunged against the leash, it slipped from Julie's slack grip. Julie spun, crying out as her pet made a dash for something—maybe one of the feral cats she often saw hanging out in alleys behind the hotels. A horn blared. Tires squealed on the asphalt pavement. Screaming, Julie bolted after her pet. A black SUV bore down on them. Noodles was surely going to die. She was going to die too. The driver screeched to a halt mere inches from her frozen body. Unable to make herself move, she stood, trembling, her eyes closed. She'd survived, but no way could the driver have missed hitting Noodles.

"Lady, get the fuck out of the road," the driver yelled. "What are you, crazy?"

"I'm…I'm sorry." Julie tried to move, but her legs wouldn't obey her brain. Oh, God, she couldn't bear looking. Seeing Noodles smashed on the pavement.

A strong arm encircled her waist, tugged her out of the path of the vehicle. "Be on your way, man. Can't you see the lady is in shock?" The voice surrounded Julie like a caress. A voice like the mellow, supremely male one she'd heard inside her head last night. "This is yours, I believe?"

When she opened her eyes, she saw him. The beautiful man she'd been ogling…and Noodles, looking small, helpless and unharmed, apparently quite satisfied to be held in the crook of her savior's muscular arm. "Oh, yes. Thank you." When she reached out to retrieve her dog, their hands touched. Moisture pooled between her legs. Sexual awareness sizzled through her veins, set off by the merest hint of physical contact. Did he feel it too? "Thank you so much. I don't know if I could have stood it if I'd lost… What can I do to repay you?"

"I'm sure you'll think of something appropriate. I'm Stefan d'Argent. At your service." One eyebrow lifted, giving him a slightly sardonic expression.

"Julie. Julie Quill. And that's Noodles. Noodles, you're a bad, bad girl."

He glanced down at her dog that seemed in no hurry to leave the safety of his arms. "Noodles almost became part of the pavement out there."

"I know." Guilt washed over Julie because now, as a few moments ago, she found herself mesmerized, her body responding shamefully to the simple proximity of him. She'd nearly lost her precious pup, and all she could think about was this gorgeous man—Stefan seemed a very appropriate name—and how she imagined she'd feel if he caressed her the way he was now stroking an appreciative Noodles. "I can't thank you enough."

He set Noodles down but made no move to hand Julie her leash. "There is a way." He caught and held her gaze, and the heat that sizzled between them nearly made her jump back, take refuge in the night. "My flight arrived hours later than I planned. I'd had reservations at the Marquisa, but the manager apparently thought I'd canceled them and sold my room to someone else. You might allow me to pass the rest of the night in your guest room."

Julie didn't invite strangers in for coffee, much less to spend the night, but she found herself nodding, holding onto Stefan's hand while he held Noodles' leash. The innocent contact seemed not innocent at all—charged with sexual energy she sensed he held in tight restraints.

It was weird. As though a force outside Julie had taken over her will, made her acquiesce to this stranger's every request. As though their meeting—their future together—had been destined by some higher being. Devil or angel, she didn't know.

"Are you new to Chicago?" she asked, trying to regain some equilibrium, some sense of normalcy.

"Yes. My home is in France. From your accent, I assume you're not a native Chicagoan."

"You're right. I grew up in New Orleans. My father still lives there. I suppose I moved to spread my wings, but I miss him. Independence isn't always all it's cracked up to be." Standing there, volunteering details of her life to this compelling stranger, made no sense. It was as though some outside force had taken over Julie's brain. Filled her with feelings she couldn't understand. Compelled her to explore the sensations that had overcome her the moment she saw him.

"No. My family's very important to me. I try not to stay away from them too long. Though I've been grown for a long time, my mother still worries about me."

Ah. Here was a man who was not only gorgeous and as sexy as anyone Julie had ever met but who also cared about his family. "I'm sure she does. Come on now, admit some of your faults. Everybody has them."

He grinned. "I'm a paragon of virtue. Just ask Mama."

The French pronunciation that would have sounded so affected coming from most of her friends somehow seemed right from Stefan, though his accent was so slight Julie would almost have thought him a native-born American. She paused under a street lamp and glanced at her watch. "Oh my, you must be exhausted, and here I am keeping you up. Let's go inside and get you to bed."

When she unlocked the door, he held it open for her. "I'm a night person. You're not keeping me up at all, but please. Feel free to leave me to my devices and take to your own bed."

Julie didn't want to say goodnight to her fascinating guest. Not yet. And she didn't feel comfortable leaving him alone, awake in her apartment while she slept. "Could I fix you a late-night snack first?"

"No, thank you." He lifted her hand to his lips. "You've been too kind already."

The touch of his lips to her knuckles heated her—not just at the point of contact but throughout her body. She wanted more. What had come over her? She didn't fall in bed with every good-looking man she met. She never entertained lustful thoughts about strangers. Well, she never had, until she met Stefan.

That she yearned for him to take her boggled her nerves. Damn it, she should never have let him in, never invited him to stay. Julie told herself she'd been a fool, was even more a fool now because she knew she'd drag him to her bed if she didn't get away. She had to steel herself against whatever it was about him that seduced her senses, without him having made any overt effort to approach her sexually.

She had to recover some perspective, and it was certain she wouldn't get it standing in the same room with him. She'd scurry off to her bedroom and lock the door, as much to keep herself inside as to keep him out. "Well, I believe I'll get a little something for myself and go turn in. Tomorrow I'll give you a guided tour of the local haunts, if you'd like."

"I'll be looking forward to it." Though his touch on her hand was light, unthreatening, his gaze scalded her, hinted he'd exact far more from her if she'd allow it.

If she'd allow it? She'd welcome the touch of his large, well-shaped hands…his incredibly sensual mouth. Her panties were already soaking wet from imagining having his body on hers, in hers, thrusting his cock into her pussy again and again until she screamed with pleasure… *Face it, Julie. You want him to fuck you, more than you've ever wanted a man before.* She imagined lying in the cocoon of his arms, safe from… What on earth was she thinking about?

She'd always prided herself on being self-sufficient, on not needing a man to be complete. Why was it now, with this total stranger, she longed to have him possess her…consume her? "I'm afraid I haven't prepared very well for overnight guests," she said, surprised she'd found the strength to utter the words as she unsnapped the leash from Noodles' collar. "Until tomorrow, I'm afraid you'll have to make do with the couch."

He flashed a smile, a very white smile that revealed prominent incisors—a small, endearing imperfection that made his perfect male appearance just that much more intriguing. "I don't mind."

"You say that now. I'd put you in the guest room, but the smell of linseed oil and canvas primer would probably choke you. I just primed a new canvas in there today. Hold on, I'll bring you some bed linens so at least you'll stay warm."

Later, after they'd worked together to spread a sheet and blanket over her living room sofa, Julie bid Stefan goodnight. Instead of trotting along behind her, Noodles curled up at Stefan's feet.

Strange. While she was basically a friendly dog, Noodles didn't usually take to strangers right away. Not the way she'd latched onto Stefan. Of course, she seldom took an instant dislike for anybody the way she had this afternoon with Mr. Reynard. Julie rummaged through the kitchen for some of the fruit and yogurt her guest had declined. Maybe whatever seductive quality Stefan had that had drawn her in also had worked on her dog.

Mmmm. The yogurt hit the spot. If only it eased the needy feeling low in her belly the way it satisfied her hunger.

Still pondering the instant, nearly hypnotic attraction that had her longing to join Stefan and beg him to fuck her, Julie padded to her room and crawled in bed. Sleep wouldn't come. What if he were a psycho? No, he couldn't be. Yes, he could. She got up, crossed the room and checked the lock on the door.

Why had she done that? She wanted him to come to her. Come in her. Her need for him was primal, unquenchable by social mores. And he was here. In her house, on her living room couch, in close enough proximity that she could take a dozen steps and… No. She couldn't.

She had to. Kicking away the covers, she got up and tiptoed down the hall. He slept soundly, so soundly she couldn't make out the motion of him breathing beneath the lightweight blanket.

Apparently he needed his sleep. Not the attentions of a woman whom he'd bewitched.

Twice more she got up, intending to go to him, stopped at the last minute by the realization that what she was feeling was too much, too soon. Despite the illogical, inexplicable passion for him that sizzled through her veins, they were virtual strangers, together due to an inexplicable twist of fate.

* * * * *

He was famished. Unlike those callow youths of the d'Argent clan who'd been amusing him for months with their futile pursuit, Louis Reynard could not go for days, even weeks, between feedings. Late that night, he rose from his bed, determined to find sustenance ere morning broke, rendering him virtually impotent until the sun disappeared once more in the western sky.

Though the soft bed, clean Egyptian cotton sheets and the other amenities of the small but luxurious hotel pleased him, the lack of likely victims in its immediate vicinity did not. Noting that his present d'Argent shadow was napping peacefully on a sofa outside his room, Louis made his way outside.

He could have killed the young pup—Claude, if he recalled the sleeping vampire's name correctly. But that would have been too easy. It was not yet time to draw the ire of all the d'Argent hunters, which he'd certainly do if he destroyed one of their own. First he must marshal all the forces of his own clansmen and prepare for out-and-out vampire war. War he knew would come, once he'd left dead bodies of his victims in a macabre pattern that zigzagged around the earth. Once he'd returned to Paris and destroyed Alina as she'd destroyed his hope—his dream of omnipotence in the vampire world. His fantasy of becoming whole again.

Besides, Louis didn't relish drinking vampire blood—even blood from one of Alina's followers. Mortals' blood tasted younger, more refreshing. Only Queen Alina's own lifeblood would bring him the ultimate in gratification. As he prowled the nearly empty streets, he considered the satisfaction he'd gain, taking his next victim right under the watchful eyes of the d'Argent hunters.

The elation he'd feel when he finally destroyed them and Alina with them.

The waning moon illuminated Louis' way. He remained alert, on the lookout for a vagrant, anyone who'd not soon be missed. Far afield of the hotel now, moving under the elevated train tracks toward the Loop, he stalked a likely victim into a darkened alley, waiting for the man to pause in his search for whatever it might be he thought he'd find.

Ah. A bottle. He might have known. From the man's halting gait, Louis deduced he'd already drunk more than his share. Still, no more sober victim presented himself, and Louis was weak with hunger. Moving quickly, for the man needed no more alcohol in his blood than apparently was already there, Louis swooped down, grasped the scraggly hair on his victim's head and bared his throat. A northbound train rumbled noisily overhead, almost drowning out the clatter of glass breaking on the brick alleyway. The glass shards bombarded Louis' legs, but he hardly noticed the pain. He'd already sunk his fangs into the victim's jugular and was gorging himself on fresh, warm blood.

As he fed, Louis savored the slow, steady build-up of sexual tension that reminded him of years ago, of the pretty young virgin he'd raped the day before her father had buried him alive. His fangs sank deeper into his victim's throat. He sucked harder, seeking that blessed release that had been denied him since his death. He imagined his cock swelling, expanding, told himself he almost felt the rush toward climax...

His victim's loose, damp flesh grew cold under Louis' hands. The flow of blood slowed, then stopped. He'd sucked the man dry, but still he wanted more. More that he could never have, more that he could never hope for since Alina had turned him down. He was destined to remain a eunuch, to be denied even a vampire's satisfaction from his feedings.

Disgusted, Louis let his victim go. The bum sank to the ground with a thud. Dead. Louis straightened, stared down at the empty husk of a mortal, then shook the shards from the shattered bottle out of the cuffs of his custom-tailored slacks.

No one would miss this creature, another hapless drunk, a street person whose rancid body odor mingled with the stench of the rotgut whiskey he'd dropped when Louis had attacked.

Louis himself felt a bit tipsy. Following the elevated tracks, he retraced his steps to the hotel, shuddering when his gaze caught a pair of crosses etched into the double doors of a church he passed along the way. Suddenly reeling, he shut his eyes tightly, staggered as quickly as he could past the repugnant symbols.

Damn the d'Argents and their immunity to all things Christian that were anathema to the vampires of his own clan. Damn their ability to move about in the light with relative impunity. Damn their very un-vampirelike ability to copulate and procreate much as mortals did. Fuck every one of them. Especially the beautiful Alina d'Argent. She shouldn't have laughed at him when he'd asked her to merge their clans.

More important, Alina shouldn't have become so angry she lost her renowned composure and told him he didn't have the tools to keep her satisfied, or the means for using them.

Why couldn't she have buried the centuries-old feud? They could have been happy together, two powerful vampires, joint heads of two ancient vampire clans. Louis stumbled a little but quickly righted himself. The drunk must have imbibed even more than Louis had thought.

The liquor was making him maudlin. Baring his fangs at a growling dog, he thought back on the women he'd destroyed, savoring the knowledge that every time he killed another beautiful blonde woman, he made Alina suffer. The d'Argents had always been cursed with too strong a sense of social obligation, a weakness that had cost them their elders one by one, left the clan in the hands of the relatively young and foolish Alina.

The beautiful Alina. The memory of her gorgeous face had inspired him to search the Earth for her surrogates, surrogates to feed his hatred as well as his flesh. The thought of her blonde hair, the perfection of her features inspired Louis now as he made his way back to the hotel. Stumbling, he cursed. Quickly, he righted himself and continued on his way, concentrating on his next victim, the beauty he'd met in the park at sundown. Julie Quill. Tall, lithe, with hair like pale corn silk and a smile he imagined stole mortal men's breath, Julie looked so much like the bitch vampire queen, Louis knew he couldn't wait until the full moon to consume her. Destroy her. He'd catch his pursuers unaware, take Julie under the crescent moon. Once more he'd show Alina he possessed powers superior to that of the determined young d'Argent hunters she'd sent to bring him down. Power to destroy all she held dear.

Just five more days. He'd do it now but for the centuries-old superstition within his clan of taking significant action only on one of the four lunar cycles. With luck, the d'Argent vampire hunter he imagined would now be patrolling the lobby of his hotel wouldn't figure out in time that Louis had changed his pattern. And Louis would have struck another blow for Reynard, another against the snobbish d'Argent clan.

The last of the hunters Alina sent had gotten too close for comfort though. Louis was grateful that one was out of the picture for now, and that Alina had sent the very young son of Alain, founder of the d'Argent clan. The boy vampire had barely challenged him in Buenos Aires—had never before gone after him alone. Still, it didn't matter if the other one returned. It didn't matter if they all returned. He could defeat any of them. All of them.

Alina deserved to suffer. More than that, she deserved to die. No woman, vampire or mortal, turned Louis Reynard down and lived to tell about it. Not for long. Sooner or later, he'd catch Alina away from the faithful followers who surrounded her. When he did, he'd destroy her as surely as she'd trampled his dream of merging their two powerful clans and restoring his manhood.

He'd destroy the hunters who protected her on his own timetable. First he'd demoralize them by carrying on his bloody quest for vengeance under their very noses. Then he'd snatch Alina from her guards, drain the last drop of blood from the fickle vampire queen.

"I'll be invincible." Long ago Louis had convinced himself that drinking of her blood would imbue him with her powers. "Invincible," he mumbled to the waning gibbous moon. Just then he tripped on a loose stone paver on the sidewalk and slammed down onto his knees. Letting out a string of curses in every language he knew, Louis dragged himself upright and hobbled the few additional blocks to the hotel. Damn his sot of a victim, because now he was going to have to sleep off a drunk.

He paused a moment outside the hotel's revolving door. Had to give the appearance of sobriety. Couldn't let the d'Argent pup see and capitalize on his present weakness. Squaring his shoulders, Louis stepped forward, grasped the handrail. Still trying to feign sobriety, he stared at a dark-haired young man wearing jeans and a dark sweater as they passed through the revolving door.

Through the haze of alcohol, he searched his memory. There was something familiar...yes, that was it. The eyes. Clear, green. Not cool, but smoldering with emerald fire. D'Argent eyes. This must be another of the Young Ones. It wasn't Alexandre, the reckless youth who'd challenged him in a vampire bar in Argentina, apparently under the illusion that silver bullets would have done him in. And it wasn't Stefan, who'd had him staked the other night in Atlanta and would have destroyed him if not for his terrible aim. Louis strained his seriously impaired memory for a name. Claude. Youngest son of Alain, founder of the d'Argent clan. He'd been in Buenos Aires with Alexandre, had spirited that one away before Louis could finish him off.

Bumbling fools, every one of them. They'd been chasing him halfway around the world, but he kept on outsmarting them. "You won't get me, y'know." The words came out slurred, even to Louis' own ears. "I'm Reynard. The wily fox."

The young vampire's steady gaze seared Louis' back as he stumbled toward the elevator. Bile rose in his throat, the taste of fear. In his present state, he'd be no match for even the youngest and weakest of the d'Argents. Nausea rose, threatened to spill from his lips. He couldn't fight, so he darted from the hotel through a handy fire door.

He allowed a moment's regret for the comfortable bed he'd been anticipating but decided it prudent to disappear for now, in case his shadow decided to challenge him.

Chapter Four

ରୁ

"What?" Stefan sat up on the sofa in Julie's living room, his ears still ringing from the shrill bell on his cell phone when Claude began to talk, his speech broken up by hard breathing, as though he were a human who'd just run in a marathon. "You say Reynard came back to the hotel and then left again?"

"Yes. I lost him somewhere between the hotel and the south entrance to Lincoln Park. Thought you'd want to know. Sorry about the cell. I'm still not great at initiating mind-to-mind contact."

"Thanks." What time was it? Stefan glanced out the window, saw dawn had not yet broken. Streetlights cast eerie shadows on the tree-lined boulevard. From a distance away came a rumble from a passing commuter train. Otherwise all was quiet. "Did you say Reynard was drunk?"

"Looked like it to me. When he came into the hotel, he was staggering all over the place. Must've fed on somebody who'd just tied one on." Claude paused, as though considering the scene. "I guess he must have recognized me just as he was about to go into his room, because he ducked out an emergency exit. I should have been quicker. I might have been able to tail him."

"You're not the only one who's let the bastard slip through your hands." Stefan had thought he saw a Reynard look-alike when he'd noticed a drunk staggering down the street in front of the hotel, but apparently it had been Reynard himself. No matter. His mission had been—still was—to keep Julie safe. "Come meet me outside Julie's house. I want you to guard her for a little while. After I return, you can go on back to the hotel, get a room and rest up. Reynard will return once he's recovered. I'll need you in fighting shape later."

After he hung up, he moved quietly, opened Julie's bedroom door. Though he'd have given a hundred years of life to get Reynard in his clutches, Alina was right. The key to defeating the wily vampire was protecting Julie. By doing so, they could catch their prey unaware when he went on the attack.

Wherever the bastard was now, chances were he'd be sleeping off his indirect overindulgence. Pity Stefan couldn't read Reynard's mind when he was asleep. Disappointed that he couldn't locate and destroy the killer in his weakened state, Stefan at least was reassured that for the time being Julie was safe. He dressed, pocketed the key to the patio door and let himself outside. He wouldn't be gone more than an hour at most, would be back long before Reynard could have slept off his drunk. Not wanting to leave Julie for a moment longer than necessary, Stefan walked briskly toward Lincoln Park. He'd feed then return before Julie awakened.

There was Claude, his face visible among the sparse leaves on a shrub across the street. "Where are you going?" he whispered.

"To feed."

"Thought you just came back from Paris."

Stefan grimaced. "I did."

"Let Julie get to you, did you? She is one hot mortal chick." Claude's fangs gleamed in the moonlight when he grinned.

Smart-mouth seventy-five-year-old kid. But Claude was right. Julie was so hot, she'd gotten his usually cool blood to simmering through his veins. That had caused him to burn off energy—energy he needed intact to confront Reynard. "For a newlywed, you're awfully observant of other women."

"Marisa won't mind if I look. And I'll lay odds you'd fight me if I wanted to touch."

"You'd be right about that." Stefan shouldn't have let himself become so aroused. If he hadn't, he wouldn't be famished now, desperate to find a likely source of nourishment. Chicago's Gold Coast apparently had no vampire bars. None he'd been able to find, anyway, and he'd looked all along Rush Street yesterday. Jazz and blues bands had warred with each other in crowded clubs, where all they served was beer and liquor — and solid food of every imaginable description. Mortals' nourishment.

Too bad Stefan wasn't all that familiar with Chicago. And that he hadn't been able to think of a fellow clansman who was, at least not quickly enough to dope out area food sources. Too bad that, unlike humans, vampires didn't compile and share useful information — such as where, in a strange city, to find nourishment without resorting to feeding direct from the source.

Stefan visualized a vampire database — a travelogue of sorts. Perhaps at some point he'd put one together, share it on the Internet. No, of course he wouldn't. Neither would any other vampire, as long as there remained a strong likelihood that such a list might be obtained and used by people who thought all vampires ought to be eradicated.

Only two days ago, Stefan had drunk his fill. Now he had to feed again, and he dared not leave Louis unwatched for long enough to return to Paris and *Les Sang des Rosiers*. He dared not even leave his prey long enough to search more of Chicago for a bar that catered to his kind. Not now, when he felt certain Louis intended to strike again in four short days.

"Claude, you're certain you smelled alcohol as well as blood on Reynard?"

"Positive." The younger vampire shook his head. "I told you he could barely walk. Thought for sure I had him until he disappeared right before my eyes."

"It's all right. We'll get him. Meanwhile, I want you to stay here and watch Julie's house while I'm gone. Call me if she goes out or anyone tries to go in." With that, Stefan took off for the park, jogging easily in the pale light of dawn.

Reynard must have found an unsuspecting drunk in an alley somewhere and drained his victim dry. Stefan shuddered. When he imagined his adversary awakening many hours from now with the hangover from hell, though, he felt a fiendish sense of satisfaction.

He tipped his baseball cap to a pair of Chicago cops making early morning rounds through the park. A couple of early morning joggers passed him, sweat already soaking the lightweight T-shirts and shorts they wore. Perhaps he could delay, find a vampire bar somewhere…

No. He loathed the mere idea of feeding from a mortal, but he had to keep up his strength. Stefan pictured Julie, so beautiful, so vulnerable, as she'd been when he looked in on her moments earlier. She was depending on him. For Julie—and for Alina—he could do this.

He'd wait until he encountered a lone jogger, in an area where there would be no witnesses or unexpected visits from the patrolling officers. No need to attract undue attention. Winding pathways snaked off either side of the park's main jogging path, some shaded by ancient elms, others open to the sun. Stefan chose a narrow jogging trail curtained by the lush spring growth of bright-green elm leaves, set himself an easy pace, just another jogger doing his morning route. He spied his prey, though he winced at the thought. A male. Young and healthy-looking, a fellow runner.

Stefan delved easily into his potential victim's mind. And saw hunger. The mortal was fantasizing about a huge, succulent breakfast, the kind of meal Stefan had observed that many American mortals favored—stacks of bacon, fried eggs and a huge pile of pancakes garnished with glistening, sticky syrup. The other man's thoughts weren't all that different from Stefan's, except that he was anticipating having a small, quick feed on the other man's blood.

Salivating, yet hating the necessity of doing this, Stefan again wished desperately for a vampire bar, a blood bank, any source of blood that would allow him to satiate his hunger without sinking his fangs into the throat of an unsuspecting human. Perhaps Alina had been right. He *had* become too fastidious. Too accustomed to the rites of civilization to feel comfortable drinking from the bottle, so to speak.

This time, preying on a victim could not be helped. Stefan increased his pace, overtook the jogger and moved easily along beside him until he spied a shaded bench. He made eye contact, giving a gentle push to the man's mind so he'd overlook the abruptness of the suggestion and the fact that his own jeans and shirt were hardly typical jogging attire. "Want to take a few minutes' break?"

"Sure. Why not?"

Stefan's companion favored him with a grin that turned his blood cold. Fuck, he'd inadvertently hit on a guy with a taste for men. For him, he surmised from the glittery look in the mortal's eyes. Not that Stefan had anything against gay men—he had a couple of gay vampire buddies back in Paris—but that wasn't his taste at all. He couldn't help noticing that the man's pale blue eyes almost matched the jogging suit he wore.

Hunger warred with a reluctance to have such intimate contact with another male, vampire or mortal. Hunger won. Matching his victim's smile with a wide one of his own, Stefan joined him on the concrete park bench and slipped an arm around the mortal's broad, muscular shoulders.

The man laid a hand on Stefan's thigh, too close to his crotch for Stefan's comfort. "My name's Keith."

"Stefan." Keith was having visions of them both naked, Stefan bending him over the bench, his hand stroking Keith's spine, down toward his ass. Now he was imagining Stefan dropping his pants, putting on a lubricated condom, ramming his cock up Keith's eager ass... Deliberately, Stefan shut down his reading of Keith's mind. Some of the man's thoughts he'd rather not know. Keith would have no memory of this encounter once it was over. Because Stefan would remember, he wanted to make it short and sweet. "Come closer. I want to taste you."

Some of that same wave that drove Keith came over Stefan, affected him, reminded him of the sensual pleasure of feeding on warm human blood. He'd almost forgotten, had made himself forget that surge of erotic pleasure, the ability feeding gave to feel the soul and essence, the beauty, of one's victim...one's mate. Julie. No. Not Julie, but a stranger chosen only to quench an unholy thirst.

Keith moved with unseeming haste to accommodate him, and as Stefan zeroed in on a pulsating vein in Keith's throat, a hand moved to fondle his genitals through the rough denim fabric of his jeans. It felt weird—but surprisingly arousing. For the first time in his four hundred fifty-some-odd years of life, he was getting a hard-on for another male.

You don't want this. You want to feed, not to enjoy it. Remember, it's your own fault you're out here feeding on a mortal. If you'd fought the arousal last night, blocked out those lusty thoughts about the woman you're here to protect, you could have gone at least another week without feeding.

A small voice in Stefan's head reminded him his victim deserved a climax, so he splayed one hand over Keith's broad chest and scissored his fingers over a nipple. When Keith moaned with apparent pleasure and squeezed Stefan's cock a little harder, Stefan slid his hand lower, returned the favor through the other man's soft exercise pants. He caught his index finger in a ring that protruded from the end of Keith's rigid flesh. Damn. Putting that thick, heavy ring through his cock head must have hurt like hell. Stefan couldn't help admiring Keith for having endured what he himself couldn't imagine doing solely to adorn his genitalia. He caught the ring in the material and gave it a little tug before he resumed stroking the distended flesh it decorated.

Stefan breathed in the fishy air off Lake Michigan then sank his fangs into a pulsating vein in his victim's neck. The sensuality of feeding this way after so many years nearly overcame him. He had to take care. Mindful of the danger of gorging himself—danger to his victim, not himself—he drank moderately, trying to squelch the sexual high that threatened to make him hard as stone beneath his victim's searching hand. As he lifted his face from Keith's throat, he felt Keith's hand go limp, fall away.

Gently, for Stefan had no wish to hurt the mortal who'd just fed him, he laid Keith out on the bench, hands folded over his chest. When the man awakened in a few minutes, Stefan would be long gone. The only souvenir Keith would have of their encounter would be two faint, pink fang marks. Stefan doubted he'd even notice them, though Keith undoubtedly would notice the semen stain on his jogging pants and wonder what manner of fun he'd missed out on.

Though it was too early for Julie to be rising, Stefan headed back toward her. The eagerness with which he was looking forward to being in her company again told him that, unfortunately, this might not be his last early morning foray into the park.

Chapter Five

೫

Stefan could barely wait to see Julie again. Every cell in his body ached at the prospect of seducing her. Before he rounded the corner, he spied Claude. His young helper still stood right where Stefan had left him, concealed better now behind a full evergreen shrub.

"Not a sign of Reynard. Or anybody else for that matter. Julie's still in bed, sound asleep," Claude reported, his expression earnest.

"That's good. Thanks for keeping watch," Stefan commented. "Go on back to the hotel, call your bride and then get some sleep."

Claude shook his head, dropped his gaze for a moment to stare at his feet. "Okay. Will do. It's almost morning anyhow. And late enough that Marisa should be stirring. It's only been a day, and already I miss her."

"Young love." Though the words came out lightly, Stefan couldn't manage to stifle the momentary twinge of envy that Claude had found—and changed—his mortal lover at the tender age of seventy-five, while he was still alone at six times Claude's age. "Go on. Call her. I know you must be pining away."

Stefan parted ways with Claude and slid in through Julie's patio door. Stretching out on the sofa, he tried to summon Alex telepathically. Stefan located him with no difficulty, but it soon became evident Alex was too involved to zero in on Stefan's brain waves.

He might have known his cousin would be chasing some hot young female around the *Marais* district of Paris. He'd most likely headed there the moment his mother had agreed to let him out of bed, if for no other reason than to use his legendary prowess with women to prove himself fit. He'd be chafing at the bit to get Alina's permission to leave Paris, come to Chicago and return to the hunt.

Stefan couldn't blame him. Sometimes with Claude's assistance, Alexandre had tracked Louis from Melbourne to Buenos Aires with several stops in between. Even if he hadn't tangled with Reynard and taken a vicious beating in the process, he'd still have needed a break. Stefan imagined Alex was more than ready for some release of pent-up sexual energy. When he'd been Alex's age, Stefan had indulged his raging libido at every opportunity until the day he'd destroyed Tina with his unbridled lust.

The way he now feared he'd do with Julie unless he held himself in check. No, he wasn't the impulsive boy he'd been with Tina. He could skim his hands over Julie's warm, satiny flesh. He could arouse her, seduce her, eat her sweet cunt and fuck her — without giving in to the temptation to sink his fangs into the slowly pulsating vein at her throat and take more.

The hell he could.

But he had to.

He had to save her from himself as well as Louis. Had to keep in mind her mortality, her vulnerability to the most base of his desires. No matter how difficult it would be — and he imagined it would be practically impossible — he had to restrain himself from tasting her sweetness, mingling her mortal blood with his own.

Because with her, he sensed he wouldn't be able to stop with just a sip.

Stefan closed his eyes, but sleep eluded him. Restless, yet too exhausted to attempt mind-to-mind communication again at the moment, he fished his cell phone from his valise and put in a call to Alina. "I need Alex here. Claude's doing well — very well considering he's had so little experience at the hunt. But we're going to need our best if we're to put an end to the Fox. That's Alexandre. If he's well enough."

Alina sighed. "Alex has escaped his sickbed. At the moment, he's thoroughly enjoying his R&R. My spies tell me he's holed up with a *dhampir* stripper named Madeleine. You may know her."

Stefan did. The stripper's best-known attribute was an ability to give head that was unsurpassed by any other woman in the pleasure palaces of Paris. "Hope she doesn't sink those fangs of hers too deep." He'd never had any particular desire to let a vampire lover feed on that part of his anatomy. True, he healed quickly, like all of his kind. Still, the idea of having sharp objects buried in the sensitive flesh of his cock made him cringe. His cock stirred and hardened, however, when he imagined Julie sucking it in between her soft, mortal lips, swirling her tongue over him and nipping him gently with her glistening white teeth.

Alina chuckled. "Alex can take care of himself, I'm sure. I know you need him there. He wants that too." Her tone suddenly turned serious. "I just don't want to risk him. Let's make sure he's recovered fully. When he has, I'll send him to you."

"Thanks. If I read Reynard right, he plans to strike this time on the crescent. That's just four days from now." Stefan pictured Julie, imagined her laid out like the woman he'd discovered in Atlanta, cold and dead. Dead beyond restoring, even to the eternity of darkness that was the vampire world. His world. "Damn it, how does the bastard shield his thoughts whenever the notion strikes him? I can't read him the way I read most mortals. Or most other vampires. Alina, I cannot fail this time."

"This woman has touched you, more than any of the others." It wasn't a question but a statement, proof that his cousin and queen had powers of empathy that exceeded that of any other vampire of their clan. Powers that far outpaced his own considerable telepathic gift. "Take care, Stefan. I will summon Alex and decide for myself whether he's as fit as he seems. Some of my spies tell me he still tires easily, despite his best efforts to prove otherwise."

"Please be sure he's recovered sufficiently to come back into the field. I wouldn't want him to come to harm because he wasn't back in fighting form."

"Of course. I would no more risk Alexandre than I would you or Claude. Is your cheek healing properly?"

Stefan reached up, touched the still-angry vampire bite. Because he didn't want to alarm Alina, he casually told her, "It's coming along."

"All right. Take care of yourself. And tell Claude his mother and I have been showing Marisa the sites of Paris. And the shops." Stefan visualized Alina grinning when she made that last comment.

"I will. Thank you." Tucking the phone in his pants pocket, Stefan considered his options. Restless, he paced then sat. Finally he lay down and drifted off to sleep. A few hours later, he woke and called Claude.

"Start searching for Reynard. He should be recovering by now from his drunken stupor."

"Okay," Claude said.

Stefan yawned. Ordinarily he'd be sleeping another hour or two, but when he lay back on the couch, sleep wouldn't come. Finally, he got up, showered, shaved and dressed — and looked in on Julie.

He panicked when he didn't find her in her bedroom. Cursing, he forced himself to be still. Concentrating hard, he reached out and looked for her with his mind. And relaxed when he found her.

He followed her mental trail, and Noodles, to the doorway of her studio. Once there, he stopped, not wanting to disturb the picture she made.

Her expression serious, she stood in her studio, the strap of a silky blue nightshirt slipping down along her slender shoulder. Apparently she was engrossed in the task of restoring the painting of a buxom nude, perched on an easel by the window. Noodles waddled across the room and flopped at her

71

feet, but Julie didn't seem to notice. She wielded a slender brush in one hand, dipping it onto a palette she held easily in the other hand. Though Stefan recognized the value of the old painting, he found the artist far more arousing. Her pale hair gleamed in the morning light, a perfect contrast with her sun-kissed golden skin. He liked the way the tip of her tongue slipped out of her mouth from time to time, dampening her upper lip as she concentrated on her work.

"I see you finally woke up," she said when she noticed his presence.

He leaned against the doorframe, checking out the painting. "Eighteenth century, isn't it?"

She lifted a brow, as though surprised he knew. "Yes. Not one of the Masters, though. It belongs over the bar at a club on Rush Street. The owner hired me to restore it because some of the colors have faded badly."

"You're good. Go ahead. Don't let me disturb you. I have some calls I need to make." Stefan wandered around Julie's house, reminding himself with every bright wall he saw, each piece of evidence a mortal lived here, that his job was to protect her — as much from his own lust as from Reynard's vicious intent. Julie's little dog trailed after him, seeking attention.

"Come on, Noodles, I think I saw a ball outside that we can play with."

Noodles barked then trotted to the patio door, her tail beating out a happy rhythm as she waddled along. The fact that the dachshund seemed fond of him puzzled Stefan, because in his experience most animals steered clear of him. Of all vampires.

He'd exerted no particular influence on the dog. Come to think of it, he hadn't utilized very much of that special vampire skill on Julie, either, since they'd awakened this morning. Once he'd influenced her to invite him into her home, it seemed she'd just accepted his presence there, as though her subconscious knew and accepted that he knew best, had her best interests at heart.

"Come on, girl." Stefan followed Noodles outside, stopping beneath the roof overhang to avoid the direct sunlight. When the dog barked, as though asking what he was waiting for, he picked up a small soft rubber ball and rolled it across the flagstone patio. Noodles trotted after it, bit into it and brought it back. Proud of herself, she dropped it at Stefan's feet and let out an exuberant woof.

The revelation that he hadn't needed to use his special skill to influence Julie niggled at his mind. What did it mean? Was this a sign that fate somehow had destined that they be together, utilizing powers beyond his or her control? Unlikely.

Still, he could come up with nothing more plausible, no more than he could explain to himself why one short-legged red dog who'd hated Reynard on sight—a typical reaction to vampires that Stefan himself had experienced on occasion with other canines—had immediately realized he was friend, not foe.

Noodles jumped up on Stefan's leg, the ball in her mouth. From her quizzical expression, he guessed she was wondering why he'd invited her outside if he didn't want to play. He bent and scratched behind her floppy ears. "Sorry, Noodles. Here. Go get it." Then he tossed the ball again.

While Noodles retrieved it, Stefan shaded his eyes with one hand. His eyes burned, so much he fished out his dark glasses and put them on. Although the sun was sinking in the western sky among majestic buildings that bore marks of well-kept age but not antiquity, its rays were still intense. They reminded him of Julie's brilliant smile, of the fact she thrived in light, not darkness.

Everything reminded him of Julie. How could he seduce her without himself being seduced?

He had to. And he knew it would hurt, wanting so badly what he must not allow himself to possess. He'd give Julie pleasure, take a pittance for himself. He'd spend untold sleepless days, aching for the complete satisfaction he dared not experience. It would nearly kill him not to claim her.

Turning toward her kitchen door, he faced her, faced the danger he sensed lurked in her willing arms and in his own emotions.

He'd do what he had to, although he didn't know how he'd survive.

* * * * *

Julie had thought Stefan handsome when she first saw him, but she couldn't tear her gaze from his face now as they prepared to go out for the evening and explore her neighborhood. He'd fit so comfortably into her home throughout the day, she'd barely given a thought to him being there. She'd worked through the morning while he slept. After noon, he'd watched her work for a while. Though he'd declined her offer of a late lunch, he'd kept her company while she had a sandwich, and let Noodles entice him out onto the patio for a few minutes' play. She felt completely at ease with him, as it seemed he did with her, as though they were old friends...or lovers. Their instant connection was oddly perfect in its intimacy.

His eyes weren't brown, as she'd guessed last night, but green. Pure, clear green, neither aqua nor flecked with brown. Unique. "You have gorgeous eyes. It's a crime that you keep them hidden behind those glasses."

"My eyes are very sensitive to light." He smiled, as though this wasn't the first time somebody had commented on his twinkling eyes. He held her gaze, apparently not noticing Noodles until she rubbed against his pants leg and let out a yelp for attention. "Ah. It seems I've made another friend. She likes to fetch that ball out on the patio."

"Yes. She's apparently decided you're all right."

Stefan looked a bit taken aback, but he bent and stroked Noodles, laughing when she began to wiggle with pleasure.

"Hmmm." As though still uncertain of the dog's approval, he held his palm out so Noodles could sniff him. "It's unusual for dogs to take to me this way."

"Maybe it's because you saved her life last night." Julie had trouble imagining any female, human or canine, not taking to Stefan d'Argent. He drew her like a magnet, warming her insides better than a roaring fire in the grate, making her nipples pucker as though she were outdoors naked during a snowstorm. If they didn't leave now to explore the neighborhood the way she'd promised they would, she didn't think she could restrain herself from touching his handsome face, learning the contours of his muscular body. She already felt like ripping off her clothes and his, and dragging him down onto the plush carpet right there in the foyer.

"Well, Noodles, tell your new friend goodnight. You can't go with us." Julie handed Stefan the vintage hand-painted silk shawl she'd been holding. When he draped it around her shoulders, his hands lingered, strong and capable, surprisingly cool against her upper arms. She couldn't help it. She reached up, covered those hands with her own as she looked into his mesmerizing emerald eyes.

Sexual awareness — need — flowed between them, electric in its intensity. But there was more. An unspoken, mutual connection she sensed had begun in their respective cradles but had lain dormant until the moment they met. God, but his simplest touch had her pussy growing damp, her nipples tingling. "Shall we go?" she asked. If they didn't, she'd certainly embarrass herself.

"Let's." His smile revealed those gleaming white teeth she'd noticed the night before. Perfectly straight, with prominent incisors that added a bit of individuality but did nothing to spoil the masculine perfection of his face. For some reason, she thought about the vampires that were now supposedly accepted in American society. She'd never seen one herself. Though accepted, it was rumored they kept very low profiles, and almost like the gay community some years ago, they chose to reveal themselves only in cautious ways.

Was Stefan a vampire? He was certainly dark enough and sexy enough to fit the mold of the vampire lovers Julie had read about in fantasy romances. What if he swept her into his arms, seduced her, carried her away to his dark, dangerous castle, a prisoner of love for all time?

Oh, Julie. Get a grip. You're acting like a star-struck teenager.

He opened the door, his smile morphing into a dangerous, forbidding frown when he handed her the vase of white roses someone had left there. "Who sent you those?"

She picked the card off and opened its small envelope, smiled, then looked up into the very forbidding, dangerous eyes of Stefan d'Argent. She almost stepped backward, but he had already reached out and plucked the note from her hand. "It's from a gentleman I met in the park yesterday. He's thanking me for my kindness last night. I spoke to him a bit when I was walking Noodles," she explained, watching Stefan's expression grow even darker. "I think he was just a lonely businessman, staying at the Marquisa Hotel. That was nice of him, don't you think?"

"Nice, indeed." The words came out practically like a growl.

"I didn't see him today while I was walking Noodles, so I guess he must have finished his business."

"I wish," Stefan muttered.

Julie reached up and touched his cheek. "It's a bit premature to start getting territorial," she said, trying to inject some lightness into the moment, although she knew it wasn't premature at all. Sexual awareness crackled between them, so strong she couldn't chalk it up to her artist's natural admiration of masculine beauty. Apparently Stefan felt that connection, too. "Besides, they're only flowers."

He scowled. "Of course. Let's be on our way." In a gesture she couldn't help seeing as a sign of none-too-subtle possession, he planted his hand firmly at the small of her back as they made their way down the sidewalk.

Moonlight caught Julie's hair, gave its strands a golden glow. The ends curved inward, swayed slightly in the breeze, occasionally brushing her jaw the way he itched to do. Fine tendrils caressed the slender column of her throat, pale against the silky black background of her shawl, holding Stefan's gaze, taunting him. He tried hard not to salivate, to recall his mission was to protect, not consume and very possibly destroy the woman Louis had marked as his next victim.

He could seduce Julie in order to save her. He could. He could then walk away, leaving her with nothing but a vague memory of him in the deepest reaches of her mind. Leaving her would be hard for him, he knew.

Much more difficult than he'd imagined before meeting her. For the first time in years—almost two centuries—he genuinely wished he could crawl inside a lover's mind and stay there. Become part of her mortal life and take her with him into his own world. Stefan had the feeling that when he left Julie, he'd leave behind a large part of himself.

Thinking about the vase of roses Reynard had sent her incensed Stefan. How could the bastard have been so heartless as to send her those beautiful roses, a gesture that bore silent testimony to his murderous intent? The inexplicable pangs of hunger that racked his own belly filled him with self-loathing, because that hunger wasn't for sustenance but for the sensual pleasure of tasting Julie. Possessing her. He told himself it was the night and their proximity, the danger from which he'd been charged with protecting her. But he was fairly certain he was indulging in self-deception of the worst, most dangerous sort.

Who but a eunuch could fail to be stirred at the sight of her, bathed in moonlight while the bright neon signs of upscale clubs lent her sun-kissed skin a surrealistic glow? Though Stefan resisted it, his cock grew painfully hard as the evening wore on. Touching her, warming his hand on the silk-draped curve of her hip…feeling the intimate heat of her fingertips through the thin fabric when she tucked them into the back pocket of his slacks...listening to the lilting sound of her soft voice when she pointed out her city's landmarks...had him primed and ready. He ached with hunger for what he must not take.

Always sensitive to his surroundings, Stefan tried to tell himself it was the moonlit night, the flashing neon and soulful jazz music that wafted to his ears from one of the clubs along Rush Street, putting him on sensual overload. But he knew that wasn't entirely true. While his mind registered the signs blinking red and green, blue and purple and gold, flashing names like Mario's and Dublin Pub and Syn and Pippin's, his body heated in response not to them but to every stroke of Julie's fingers on his forearm, searing and arousing him even through the layers of his clothes.

"You know, I haven't seen you nibble on the snacks or take more than a sip from your drinks anywhere we've stopped," Julie said suddenly. "You must be famished. I know this little retro diner down by the river that serves some of the best omelettes you ever ate. Would you like for me to take you there?"

Stefan tried not to fixate on the throbbing pulse in her throat. "I have somewhat eccentric feeding habits. If you're hungry, of course we can go there."

She stopped beneath a streetlight, turned on her heel to face him. He kept her hand, and she slid her free one onto his chest, curled into the fabric of his shirt. "I've enjoyed every moment of our time together tonight, but I need more. I need you. I can't explain it, but this feeling has been building in me until I can't bear it anymore."

It seemed natural, right, for him to make himself inhale and exhale, to steady himself as much as to enjoy feeling his flesh rise and fall against the light pressure of her fingers. He released her hand so he could cup her cheek, knowing then that he was lost.

She spoke again, her voice soft yet urgent. "What I'm really hungry for is you."

"And I for you. I've a feeling this—this need that flows between us—was destined from the start." He cupped her cheek, brushed his lips across hers, barely able to restrain himself from deepening the kiss, tasting her more fully. When she moved close enough to warm him with her body heat, his blood surged, leaving him lightheaded. Carnal need overcame caution, ballooned, robbed him of rational thought. His fingers tangled in the golden strands of her hair for he dared not draw her closer, show her graphically how much he wanted her. Not here, underneath a streetlight at the corner of Rush and Oak Streets, in plain view of any merrymakers who might chance to leave their favorite watering holes at just this moment.

He dared not break the gentle kiss, for if he did, he feared he wouldn't be able to stop himself from tasting her, putting her at risk in a way she couldn't possibly understand. Finally Julie pulled away, tilting her head back as though offering her throat for his pleasure. Her tongue darted out, apparently eager to taste him on her tempting, swollen lips. "Let's go back to my house."

Stefan gazed into her beautiful eyes and then he knew he'd been right all along. He'd set out to seduce her, only to find himself thoroughly seduced.

* * * * *

Her bedroom reflected who Julie was…who Stefan wasn't. Walls the color of clotted cream, moldings pristine white, satiny French doors overlooking a floodlighted patio garden through the sheerest of curtains. A huge painting of sunflowers on a dark-blue background—excellent quality, but he didn't recognize it as the work of an artist he knew—hung above a king-size bed. Glancing back at the bank of doors with clear glass panes, he imagined the morning sun bathing the spacious room in light. Light he'd find blinding if he didn't don the dark glasses he never ventured outside without during the day.

Nothing like his bedroom back home, with its deep burgundy draperies that obscured the view of the English Channel, and matching bed hangings he kept drawn to block stray sunbeams that dared to sneak past the initial barriers. No mirrors to reflect and magnify the occasional errant sunbeam, temporarily rendering him totally blind.

She'd hate your home, find it too dark, oppressive.

Not a problem, Stefan told his inner voice. That would never be an issue, no matter how much he might wish it otherwise. He didn't need his conscience to remind him of Julie's vulnerabilities. Of the danger within him that she courted so unknowingly, inviting him to take her as she'd done moments earlier.

He'd barely managed to resist showering with her when she asked. Now the sound of rushing water filled his ears, flooded his mind with images of droplets sluicing over Julie's slender throat, her ripe, full breasts. Her belly. He longed to go to her, kneel, spread her legs and lick away the moisture from her cunt. She'd taste clean, slightly salty, her fragrance of musk and roses light, never overpowering.

He'd delve into her cunt with his tongue, finger-fuck her tight little ass, drive her crazy with wanting. Then he'd wrap her in a towel, dry her warm, smooth skin, carry her to her bed and kneel over her mouth. She'd give better head than any he'd had over the centuries, sucking and licking and nipping him with her teeth while cradling his balls between her hands.

Then he'd take her cunt and her ass, and when he'd claimed her with his cock, he'd sink his fangs into her throat and…no, he must not.

With difficulty, Stefan restrained himself from joining her in the shower. He had to hold his emotions under tight rein. It wasn't enough that he protect Julie from Reynard. He must shield her from the beast that roared within himself. He could do it, must do it. Seduce her, protect her…then walk away once the risk to her was over, leaving her to her mortal pursuits. Save Julie. Save Julie. He repeated those words like a litany, over and over, until it began to sound more like the plea of a desperate man than the determined conviction of a vampire hunter.

He glanced at the painting above the bed, suddenly realizing when he noticed the bold "JQ" at the lower right corner that Julie did more than "work" with art. She'd apparently created this and many of the other striking paintings lining the rooms of her house.

He was about to seduce—compel—a mortal who fed on sunlight and brilliant colors. Not one who'd adapt well to an eternity of darkness, even if he were selfish enough to turn her. Stefan barely held back an oath. It was so damn unfair to have found a perfect mate...one who wanted him as much as he wanted her...only to have to make love to her to save her from Reynard, and then to let her go.

He toed off his shoes and rubbed his feet against plush carpeting the dark blue color of the midnight sky. As he stepped out of his slacks, he noticed the waning moon peeking between the window frames. They only had three more nights...three days. Three short days before Louis would make his move, before Julie's life would be in immediate danger and Stefan would be her only chance for survival. Three days to make memories for himself that would have to last a lifetime—in his case, many centuries during which he'd regret having lost her in his every waking hour as well as in his dreams.

In three days he'd have to be at his fighting best to meet an adversary stronger than any other he'd ever faced. An enemy stronger than himself. Fuck, but Stefan couldn't face Louis down alone. Not when Julie's life would depend on him destroying his prey.

As much as he hated to risk Claude, he'd have to depend on Alain's only living son to confront the Fox with him. And pray Alex would get here in time to help. Stefan made up his mind then that he had to swallow his pride and call Alina. He'd ask her to send several other youthful members of the clan. Perhaps numbers could negate Reynard's advantage of age, though he knew from painful experience that sometimes help from novices was worse than no help at all. Still, he had to do all he could, risk whatever he must, to save Julie and prevent other women from falling to Reynard's bloodlust.

Stefan had to have an edge. He dared not risk draining his strength in Julie's welcoming body, yet he couldn't deny her need. He'd have to tell her. Warn her of the danger she faced. Reveal himself for what he was and enlist her help in protecting herself. Perhaps she'd even help him find a likely source for fresh, life-sustaining blood other than the enticing vein in her pale, slender throat, for with his constant state of arousal, he knew he'd require a good supply.

Stefan bent, initially intending to dress before Julie finished her shower. Then he changed his mind and stripped off the rest of his clothes. Once she saw him as he'd been born centuries earlier, without the pretense of clothing, she'd have to believe he was of another species…the creature of the night mortals had feared and reviled since the earliest recorded history.

She'd look closely. Her pupils would dilate. Her lips would go slack when she saw the creature she'd thought she wanted to make love to. Seeing her revulsion—that would nearly destroy him. But it couldn't be helped. After flipping on the lamp at a bedside table he drew back the covers on Julie's bed.

In the bright circle of lamplight, she couldn't help but notice his body didn't look quite like that of most mortal males. Intending to lie there exposed to her scrutiny, he stretched out on the pale blue cotton sheet. Then, because he couldn't help himself, he drew the top sheet up over his pale, hairless chest.

One more time. Surely it wouldn't hurt for him to see desire on her beautiful face once more. Then he'd do what he must— make the confession that had sent many a mortal screaming for the nearest lawman over the years. Just for a moment, though, he'd see desire in her beautiful eyes. The desire he read now as he drifted into her mind.

Her fierce need for him fueled his own passion, as though the irresistible pull between them were a harbinger of joy, not pain. Stefan reached over and dimmed the lamp to a soft glow.

Chapter Six

❧

Eyes to drown in. A cliché for certain, but the expression might have been freshly coined to describe Stefan's clear sea-green eyes. When he looked at her, she felt heat…the fire of his passion, or was it only a reflection of her own out-of-control desire? Julie stretched then spritzed her damp skin with her signature fragrance—a subtle blend of musk and roses made especially for her in Marie's Parfumerie, a tiny shop she'd discovered in New Orleans' French Quarter the last time she'd gone home to visit her dad.

"Do your magic, old lady," she murmured, recalling the wizened voodoo priestess who'd insisted the scent she'd created would enslave the man of Julie's dreams. Then, wrapping a pale-blue towel around her naked body, Julie opened the bathroom door.

And saw her dream lover waiting in her bed.

Hair as black as a raven's wing against the pale-blue pillow sham. Pure temptation—his was the face of a dark angel. Softly diffused light from her bedside lamp limned his striking features, shadowed the high cheekbones and aristocratic nose. The angry-looking laceration on his left cheek caught her eye. It lent a hint of danger, a reminder she knew little about him. That didn't matter. When she looked into his gorgeous eyes, she saw emerald fire.

Fire that drew her in and placed her under his sensual spell, even before he drew a hand from beneath the sheet and patted a spot on the edge of the bed. "Come here."

She wanted nothing more than to go to him, for him to hold her. Take her. Ease the ache that had grown in the pit of her stomach since she'd first seen him in front of the hotel. Slowly, deliberately, she unwrapped her towel and stood naked before him, an eager victim for the erotic delights he promised with that wicked, knowing smile.

His teeth flashed snowy white, made his pale skin appear almost tanned by contrast when she sat and bent to brush her lips across his. With surprisingly cool hands, Stefan framed her face. "There are things about me you don't know. Things you need to know."

"You've got a wife and six kids stashed away somewhere?"

"No, but—"

"Some dread disease?"

"Of course not."

The laceration on his face drew her attention. "Don't tell me you've done something...gotten in trouble with the law."

He shook his head. "The scratch is my punishment for a moment of carelessness, nothing more."

"Then it doesn't matter." If he didn't touch her—take her— she'd die. Her pussy throbbed. Every cell in her body burned. "I don't understand it, but I knew the moment I saw you that this was...destined."

"I knew it as well. Turn off the light and come here. Warm me." He sighed, as though resigned more than eager to fulfill that destiny.

His flesh felt cool yet satiny when she laid her head on his muscular chest and entwined their legs. He moaned when she wrapped one hand around his big, thick cock and cupped his sac with the other. His skin there was incredibly soft. Incredibly smooth.

So. He shaved his body. That must have been why he'd covered up—why he wanted no light but that faint glow provided by the lamp. "You feel so good. I've never understood why men who shave should worry that women won't like them smooth."

"I don't. Shave, that is. Except for my face. I don't grow body hair."

Unusual. She liked the smoothness of his skin, the sensation of satin over hard male muscle. She liked it a lot.

"Look at me." He slid his hand along her throat, drawing her attention to his eyes, so close now to her own. "I'm a vampire, my darling. I...my hunger for you is so fierce, I cannot bear it."

She stared up at him, something powerful pounding through her at his admission. So he wanted her so much, he could compare himself to a creature of the night in his hunger. This unexpected, poetic side of her dark angel pleased her. "Then feed on me," she whispered, arching her neck. "I want you to have all of me that you can take."

His groan, and the hard clutch of his hands on her shoulders, confused her, but a moment later he rubbed his cheek over one breast, brushing the nipple, making it tighten and sending the heat of arousal straight to her pussy. He definitely could grow a beard if he wanted to. She loved feeling that sandpapery rasp of stubble against her own tender skin.

Touching his incredibly smooth sac, feeling his heavy testicles shifting beneath her fingers, running her hand along the rigid length of his cock...she'd never felt anything so hard and yet so smooth to the touch. Her mouth watered at the thought of taking him, tasting him. She had to sample him with her tongue. She nipped her way down his chest, tonguing his navel briefly before sliding down, dropping kisses along the underside of his cock, swirling her tongue around the incredibly soft skin of his corona. He tasted incredibly clean, as though he never sweated.

"Come here. I want to taste you too."

He turned her, lifted her, stroked along her flanks as though memorizing their contours. As if he loved the sensation of touching her, stoking her flames as she knelt over his face. His hands slid higher, his touch so gentle it seemed almost reverent. Yet arousing. When would he touch her intimately?

Now. He took his thumbs and opened her. Cool air made her shiver, but not for long. When he slid a finger along her wet slit, seeking, arousing, finding her clit and tonguing it, he seared her with his heat, his passion. He sucked her quivering flesh into his mouth while he stroked her sides, seeking and finding both breasts. Both sensitive nipples. Tugging there, sucking her clit, lapping up the moisture that gushed from her needy cunt.

No man had ever made her so hot, so fast. She wanted him as needy as she, as eager to join their bodies and fuck until they collapsed in a heap of sweat and exhaustion. Cupping his testicles in one hand, she wrapped the other around the base of his cock and took as much of him as she could into her mouth. He throbbed against her throat, so big, so smooth. When she swallowed, he let out a low moan against her own swollen clit.

Everywhere he touched her with his mouth drove her higher. Each sensuous slide of his tongue over her pussy stoked her need. As though he knew she wanted even more contact, he pinched her nipples lightly and rubbed their aching tips against the satin-smooth skin that stretched over his washboard abs.

She needed more. Needed his huge, throbbing cock in her, stretching and filling her. Ramming into her over and over, building the pressure, bringing her to a climax like none she'd ever felt before. When she swallowed again, she felt his groan all the way to her womb. Her belly clenched. She sucked harder, ravenous for a taste of his essence. Her body arched involuntarily as the bubble of sensations burst, first deep inside her, then radiating to her swollen pussy, her breasts, everywhere any part of her touched part of him.

She'd never come so hard, so fast. Without a man inside her. God, she wanted now to taste the drop of lubrication she finally coaxed from his huge, pulsating cock. She raised her head and licked the slick, warm fluid from the tip of his cock head.

Her pussy still thrummed with aftershocks from her orgasm moments later when he shifted, positioned himself, and drove into her from behind. His big hands clutched her breasts again, kneading, stroking, building up a need for more though she'd not yet recovered from the first climax he'd given her. His hard belly slammed against her buttocks with every pistoning motion of his hips, taking her higher…making her want more. More of him.

"Oh yes, please." The harder and deeper he took her, the more she wanted of him. "Give me all of you," she whimpered. "Now. Oh, yes. You're so big. So powerful."

"So wanting to devour you, *chèrie*." He'd laid his head on her upper back—she could tell by the feel of his silky hair, the hint of evening beard growth tickling her skin. "Can't…can't hurt you, though. Never would forgive myself."

"You won't hurt me. I'm tougher than I look." Those delicious feelings were building inside her again, needing the tiniest nudge to push her over the edge to ecstasy. "Fuck me, Stefan. Fuck me hard."

He reared back, grasped her hips, pounded into her until all she could do was whimper with the pleasure-pain of it. "Yes. Like that. Oh yes."

Stefan held tight rein on his emotions. She might say she wanted him to devour her, but she didn't know. *Didn't know.* She had no idea how having her cunt, so hot and giving, surrounding his cock like a tight, slick glove, aroused him. No idea how much he wanted to consume her, claim her. Make her his for all eternity. It didn't help that she was begging him to give her more, take more. Or that with his every stroke into her sweet channel, she opened further, took all of him, wouldn't let him measure his strokes. He tightened his jaw, determined that when he came he wouldn't take her the way he yearned to do.

He would not taste her. Mark her. And he'd never give in to the need to claim her fully. Not at the risk of her life.

His balls tightened. He was close. His seed bubbled scalding hot, eager to spurt out into her waiting womb. Each contraction of her cunt around him brought him closer—closer to fulfillment. His fangs scraped his lower lip, growing, elongating, readying themselves to culminate the encounter, provide the ultimate sexual high she seemed to want so much.

No. It took a force of will he hadn't been sure he possessed, but he managed to clamp down rather than dig into her tempting flesh when her trembling climax triggered his own. The pleasure would have overwhelmed him as he spurted the essence of himself into Julie's eager body, but for the excruciating pain of his fangs piercing his own tongue.

* * * * *

"Why are you closing the drapes?" Julie asked the next morning after she'd let Noodles into the courtyard to take care of her morning toilette. She'd hoped Stefan would sleep for a while longer. He'd seemed drained last night after they made love a second time.

"Sit down, Julie." He looked disturbingly solemn, deliciously naked but for the large towel he'd wrapped around his narrow hips.

Did he regret that they'd made love? "What's wrong?" A lump formed in her throat when he took a seat not on the bed beside her but on the tapestry-covered chaise she'd found at an antique auction not long ago. Noodles deserted her, hopped up instead on the chaise, as close as she could get to Stefan.

He patted the dog when she licked his hand, then met Julie's gaze. "I spoke the truth to you last night, Julie. I closed the drapes because sunlight is my enemy. I'm a vampire."

Julie laughed then bent down to pet Noodles. "You're being silly. You scared me for a minute there."

His hand came down, took hers from Noodles. He drew it back up to hold between them, which also drew her gaze to his face.

He wasn't smiling.

"You're joking," she said, not quite so certain now.

"You know my kind lives among yours now."

"Of course I've heard of vampires. That doesn't mean I believe in them. Or that I believe you're one." Still, Julie wondered. Vampires were said to possess frighteningly strong powers of persuasion, and Stefan had certainly drawn her in, made her want...

He met her gaze, his own expression deadly serious. "Why would you not believe? Our existence has been documented through the centuries."

"All right. Say you really are a vampire, although if you are, you're very different from any vampire I've ever read about or seen in movies. Why didn't you tell me this when we met? Or before we made love?" Her words trailed off as she remembered — his touch, the heat of his hot seed bathing her womb.

Stefan reached out, took her hand. "I did tell you last night. And I had a very important reason for not revealing myself to you immediately. You are in danger, and the reason I am here is to protect you. I didn't know if you were a person who, like many, would have run in fear from me, shut yourself away from me where I could not protect you." He hesitated then parted his lips.

Julie gasped. The incisors that had seemed just a bit longer than the normal person's had elongated, so now they curved wickedly over his bottom lip. Then she blinked, and they had retracted by the time she looked again. He laid her hand carefully on his knee, withdrew his own and then lifted his lids, meeting her gaze with the expression of a man prepared to be struck between the eyes with a lethal instrument. "I want you," he said roughly. "Too much for your own good. Make no mistake about that. I'd leave now to protect you from me, but I've come here to save you from a serial killer who has you marked as his next victim. I cannot leave you as long as he's a threat."

"Please. Don't insult my intelligence. Tell me the truth about what's going on." Emotions warred inside her. Hurt, anger...and something more. Some deep, enduring emotion she wouldn't let herself accept was love. Was Stefan being deliberately cruel? Was he insane? What was going on? Why did she feel her world was spinning away off its axis, her mind and soul torn between incredulity and betrayal? She jerked her hand from his.

Julie hated the conflicting emotions that gripped her and fought hard to swallow the lump that had developed in her throat. A lump that threatened to strangle her. Though too overwhelmed to get out the words—the questions that flooded her mind—she forced herself to meet Stefan's emerald gaze. "You're...you're really a vampire?"

He held out both hands. "What do you see, Julie? Why do you think I'm so pale, and why do you imagine I have no body hair? Though I can function in daylight better than most of my kind, I must avoid direct sunlight. Looking into a mirror temporarily blinds me. Normally I do my feeding at vampire bars, but the only sustenance I require is blood. Human blood."

She backed away from him, stumbling in her haste to put some distance between them. "W-Why? How?"

He shrugged. "A mutation of genes in my family's case, or so I'm told. The mark of Elaine, I've heard it called by those of my clan who like to wax poetic. Elaine was the unfortunate young wife of a long-ago d'Argent lord who birthed a vampire babe before she died. Rollo, the baby's father, resisted the efforts of all to have him do away with his son, and so it was that the child lived and thrived. Alain d'Argent lived nearly a thousand years and fathered four sons. My father was one of twins born to Alain's first wife. Alain's third son was born over a hundred years later, and Claude, the youngest, came along shortly before Alain was destroyed while trying to protect Europe from an Austrian madman named Hitler. Claude is the only one of Alain's sons who still lives. Alina, Alexandre and I are Claude's niece and nephews, although all of us are centuries older than he."

"When?" Julie asked, trying to make sense of Stefan's abbreviated chronology.

"All this began a thousand years ago or more."

"You mean you've always been a vampire?" Gruesome scenes from late-night movies Julie had seen came back to her, of ghouls rising from their coffins at night, of handsome men shifting into bats and swooping down to feed on unsuspecting women. She'd heard stories that some of the vampires were good, not evil, but all the images that crowded her mind now came from those ghoulish movies and horror stories. "I thought vampires were created from people who'd died, and that they only come out of their graves at night."

"Yes, most humans think that. There are clans of vampires who proliferate themselves by turning those who've died. Others multiply by preying on unsuspecting humans and making them vampires. These made vampires tend to be evil, which bodes no good for the rest of us." Stefan's expression turned fierce. Frightening. His pupils dilated, so much that his eyes looked more black than green.

"So what kind of vampire are you?"

"A vampire born. A d'Argent. A hunter of evil vampires throughout Earth." He looked at her, his look softer now. "A vampire who would die before he'd hurt you. Say you don't believe I'd..." He looked as though he wanted to say more, yet could not find the words.

God, but she wanted to believe him. Still, visions of ghouls danced in her head. Stefan was no ghoul. "Of course I never believed those gruesome stories. But I don't believe you either. You're not dead. You're very much alive." Tears stung her eyes, threatened to spill over the lids and down her cheeks.

"Come here, Julie."

His tone brooked no argument. Besides, this was the same man—vampire—with whom she'd made hot, sweet love. Whose arms had held her safe and secure while they slept. Slowly, she crossed the room, stopped a foot or so from Stefan. "Well?"

"I'm not dead, but I'm not mortal either. Put your hands on my chest. Do you feel my heart beating?"

She did as he asked, felt cool flesh against her fingertips. Still flesh. None of the regular pulsing of life she expected to feel. It must have been his suggestion. This couldn't be. Telling herself not to panic, she moved her hands, seeking…feeling for the slightest movement. Anything. Affirmation that it had been a mortal being who'd taken her to heights of sensation she'd only imagined.

Her own breathing grew faster, shallow when she felt nothing, not even the coursing of his blood through the prominent vein in his neck. As though to soothe her, he covered her hands with his own, dragged them to his lips. "Do you believe me now?"

"B-but I felt you breathing. I felt your heart beating last night."

"I don't have to breathe, but I can when I choose to. And my heart does beat, but so slowly as to be virtually undetectable unless I'm feeding or aroused. Last night, Julie, I was very much aroused. I'm becoming so again, from the mere touch of your hands on my flesh, but I dare not do as my body bids me and take you again now, when I'm in dire need of sustenance."

"What…who…" She barely could speak the words. "Do you feed on living humans? Sleep in a coffin or a grave somewhere?" A horrific scene of Dracula, staked, rising from his grave, resurrected with a priest's spilled blood, flooded her memory. *Dracula Has Risen from the Grave* had given her nightmares for months after she and her friends had watched the classic horror movie one Halloween night. Scenes from that movie, of the vampire draining the blood of women, replayed in her head, taunting her. The worst thing was…Julie still ached for Stefan's touch, still longed for him to drag her to him and fuck her until they both were sated, devour her if that indeed was what he desired.

He met her gaze, held it, compelling her to listen. "Yesterday I fed on a jogger in Lincoln Park. Pierced a vein in his throat and sucked my fill of his blood."

"You killed him?" Her mouth gaped open with horror at the stark picture he'd painted in her head.

"No. He's fine. Woke up happy, without any memory of what left him feeling so good."

Julie's own blood surged with revulsion—or was it a macabre fascination? "Did—did you know Lincoln Park used to be a cemetery more than a hundred years ago? That they moved the bodies from there to Graceland because the city fathers had concerns about contaminating the water supply?"

"No. I know almost nothing of Chicago's history. I chose the park because of the privacy afforded on some of the more secluded jogging trails. Julie. Please listen. I'm not a ghoul. Graves and graveyards hold no fascination for me. When I'm not chasing vampires who'd hurt people and destroy the good names of all of us, I live in an old, comfortable home built of stone and timbers, overlooking the English Channel. I sleep there as I did here last night, in a comfortable bed." He shrugged then shot her a smile that made her heart beat faster, her nipples tingle. "My bed isn't as comfortable as I found yours, with your flesh warming mine."

"But—but you drink blood." If Julie didn't keep reminding herself, she'd be crawling on Stefan's lap, seducing him, looking for more of the pleasure he'd brought to her last night. She'd be cuddling up to him much as Noodles was doing now, resting her head on his muscular thigh. She'd be tasting his long, thick cock, stroking the satiny skin that stretched over well-toned muscles in his thighs.

"Yes, I feed on human blood. My usual habit is to take my sustenance in vampire bars or on fresh blood purchased from blood banks. I've not yet found a source here in Chicago, so I had no choice yesterday but to prey on a mortal. I left the man dazed but quite unharmed. Please believe me. Those of my clan do not destroy mortals. We are an ancient and proud family, descended from Norman noblemen who followed the Conqueror."

Julie mentally reviewed her very limited knowledge of vampire history, came up short. "Then you're from England. Or France. I thought vampires came from Romania."

"Some do. My clan hails from Normandy. The vampire who intends to kill you is of the Reynard clan, which I believe may have had its roots somewhere in Eastern Europe. The Reynards are all made vampires."

"You've mentioned 'made' vampires before. What—"

"Made vampires all were once humans. Legend has it that they originally came about when a born vampire fed on a newly dead corpse. They cannot reproduce, so they increase their numbers by that means. Only born vampires are able to reproduce in the conventional way."

A sudden chill in the air made Julie tremble. Louis Reynard? Not a kind gentleman but rather... She imagined him in a long black cloak, fangs extended, swooping down on her as she slept, spiriting her away...destroying her. No. This was all too bizarre. Too incredible.

Stefan cleared his throat. "When the moon completes its waning two nights from now, Louis Reynard will try to make you his twenty-first victim in as many months. I am here to ensure that he doesn't succeed."

Louis Reynard. The kind, gallant gentleman who'd sent her flowers as apology for canceling their meeting in the park was a vicious serial killer? A vampire? Julie's mind spun as she tried to process Stefan's words. "But—"

"If you believe nothing else I say, believe this. Four days ago in Atlanta, Reynard brutally murdered his twentieth victim. I had tracked him there but caught up with him too late to prevent another death. When I caught up to him, he was standing over her body. Blood was pooling around her from the cut in her throat. A white rose much like the ones the bastard sent you lay in her hand. Before that, the bastard had slaughtered an Argentinian heiress and eighteen more young women like her in cities and out in the countryside of every continent on earth.

"So far Reynard has eluded the best hunters of my clan. He's cunning, stealthy…appears and disappears without a trace. With each killing he grows bolder. This time he dared to provide us with your name and address, where up until now he has provided just the city…and in Atlanta, a hint as to where he'd kill his victim. I was waiting to see you, hoping for an opportunity to meet you, when I saw him approach you in the park the other evening. It was then I entered his mind, determined that he intends to kill you not on the next full moon but on the first night of the crescent."

"You entered his mind?" Stefan's story grew more incredible every moment—yet strangely Julie tended more and more to believe he was telling her the truth. Pieces of articles she'd read in the papers about the "accepted" vampires were filtering back to her. Those articles had fascinated her for a time, making her wonder what it would be like to meet a "good" vampire. What he'd be like, how he'd be different from her…

"Vampires have telepathic abilities, Julie. Some of us more than others. Mine are said to be among the best developed among the males in my clan, yet I'm unable to connect consistently with Reynard or to influence his actions at all." He shot a sheepish glance her way. "With most, mortal or vampire, I've been fairly successful at persuading them to heed my will."

Julie recalled the voice in her head that had warned her not to invite Louis Reynard into her home, and the ease with which she'd done as Stefan asked and offered him, a complete stranger, her couch the other night. "You—you used that ability to communicate with me." She didn't know whether to be furious at the blatant invasion of her mind or grateful that he'd saved her from disaster, assuming the rest of what he'd said was true.

"Yes." He paused, looked into her eyes. "I did it to protect you. Not to spy. And only at first, to get you to let me stay close to you."

Julie's head was spinning. "If what you say about Louis Reynard is true, why haven't you called the police? Why didn't you call the police in Atlanta?" Julie searched for an excuse — any excuse — to reject what her heart told her must be true. This was all too farfetched to believe — from Stefan's declaration that he was a vampire to his allegations about Louis Reynard being a vampire serial killer.

"Two of my clansmen tried doing that, in London and Brussels. They wound up in jail and had the devil's own time talking their way out. The police investigating the serial killings have started to believe they're dealing with a vampire, but they've rejected any help or involvement on our part, even tips about where Reynard may strike next. My cousin Alexandre went to the local lawmen in Montana a few months ago only to get himself locked up for a week or more as a suspect in the murder Louis had just committed at a western resort.

"They have accused those of us who tried to enlist their help of being accomplices, so now we hunt the killer on our own. And if Reynard keeps on with his killing, we fear law enforcement will conveniently forget we tried to help and blame us all. We've only recently been acknowledged in your society. We're far from true acceptance."

"Surely the FBI —"

"Your FBI and Interpol are searching for Reynard too, but they won't catch him. If they should get lucky, he'll escape from any mortal's prison. It will take another vampire to stop him. Or vampires. The Fox is nine hundred years old, with powers and cunning no younger vampire can match. Not even a born vampire." Stefan let out a sigh of frustration, bent, and fished something from the pocket of his discarded slacks.

"Assuming I believe you're a vampire…" and she wasn't sure she did, "and there has been this rash of killings…" That part seemed plausible, for she could easily research it and expose a lie. "How do I know this is for real, that this Reynard is after me, and it is not all an elaborate ruse? Or that you are not the killer?" Instinct and Noodles gave the lie to that question, but Julie wanted his reassurance.

"As for how I know Reynard has you picked to become his next victim, he sent this to Alina, queen of the d'Argent clan. Here, read it for yourself."

The folded sheet of ivory vellum slipped from Julie's bloodless fingers when she saw her name and address scripted in rusty brown letters. Script reminiscent of another time, another place. Ink that looked suspiciously like...

"Blood."

She shuddered. "Surely not?"

"Yes, he writes his notes in blood. Fitting, isn't it?" Stefan picked up the paper, stared at the lettering. "No, we don't ordinarily use blood except for nourishment."

God. He could tell what she was thinking. She wondered, just for a moment, if the letter was a fake, made up by Stefan to fool her into trusting him. No. She did trust him. So did Noodles, who'd strongly objected to Reynard but made instant friends with Stefan. "Do you always know what's in my mind before I speak?"

"Not always. Never, if I'm focusing on other things—such as the lush feel of your breasts against my chest, the incredible tightness of your cunt when it's gripping my cock." His slight smile, the twinkle in his deep green eyes, reminded her as much as his words that they'd been lovers. "I know that now you're at war with yourself, trying to decide if I'm telling you the truth or spinning an incredible tale. Come. Let's get dressed and find a library that carries newspapers from around the world. I'll show you I do not lie about the murders at very least. We can take Noodles with us for her morning walk." He scratched the sleek red fur on the dog's back then set her gently onto the floor.

"We can't take her with us. The libraries don't allow dogs inside. Except guide dogs for the handicapped." Perhaps they should. Dogs' instincts tended to be basic, not colored by the nuances of civilization. Then she remembered how Stefan had deliberately closed the drapes a few minutes earlier. "The light? Won't it bother you?"

"It will bother me, but it won't turn me into a crumbling heap of cinders. That's nothing but myth. Just as it's pure folklore that vampires sleep in coffins and require the dirt of our home ground in order to rest." He bent and stroked Noodles' silky ears. "Supposedly animals recognize us for what we are and steer clear of us. I think it's that they're able to sense good or evil intentions in every other creature. Noodles, you're a smart pup. You must sense I mean you no harm." Stefan rose, letting the towel drop to the floor. His magnificently sculpted body glowed like ivory in the filtered light from the morning sun. "Don't worry about me going outside. I often venture out in daylight, fully dressed, with dark tinted glasses to protect my eyes."

Julie's body tingled when she looked at the rippling muscles in his arms and shoulders, his rock-hard thighs and beautiful, gently curved penis and satiny scrotum. She wanted to believe him, did believe his story about the women dying. Then she remembered the roses—the white roses that had come while he slept. And the single blossom he'd seen clutched in that unfortunate victim's hand.

She did believe Stefan. And she wanted him as her lover, vampire or not. "I'd love to paint you," she said softly, her gaze steady on his perfectly made body. "I thought it the first time I saw you. I'd sculpt you from a perfect slab of *Crème Broule* or Tuscany Cream marble, if only I were competent to do you justice. Whatever, whoever you are, you're one beautiful male. I just…I don't know."

"I'm glad you find me pleasing to look at. Come, let me show you I'm telling the whole truth, that twenty beautiful women have met death at the hands of one crazed killer vampire."

Julie shrugged out of her robe and stepped over to the dresser. "Why?" she asked as she pulled jeans and a lightweight sweater from a drawer. That was the missing puzzle piece—the killer's motive for what seemed senseless acts of violence against women.

Stefan pulled on his boxers then looked over at Julie. "Why did he kill them? Revenge on all women who remind him of Alina d'Argent, queen of my clan. When Alina rejected his proposal to merge our clans, Reynard went berserk and vowed to make her regret having turned him down." Pausing, he raked her with a heated gaze. "Alina is as beautiful as you. Could practically be you, except her eyes are a clear, true green instead of the blue of a summer sky."

"Like yours."

"I suppose so. I've been told the d'Argents all share that particular trait." Stefan lifted his hand to Julie's face, traced the line of her jaw with what seemed a gentle reverence. "I can almost understand Reynard's obsession now, for it was all I could do last night to make love with you and not taste you." As though it pained him to look on her naked body and not drag her back to bed, Stefan turned away and quickly finished dressing.

It was all I could do last night to make love with you and not taste you.

Stefan's words rang in Julie's ears as she dressed, and later as they made their way down Lake Shore Drive to Congress Parkway, then west to State Street and the Chicago Central Library with its carved stone lions. He was a vampire. He'd convinced her of that much. She hadn't quite managed to persuade herself that she wasn't crazy to be encouraging him to show her the truth of twenty gory murders. Or to believe his allegation that Louis Reynard was a vampire serial killer.

All Julie knew was that she wanted Stefan d'Argent, whoever he was. As perverse, as incredibly stupid as it sounded, she wished he'd completely unleashed his passion instead of holding back to save her from himself.

Maybe she didn't want to be saved.

Chapter Seven

ઐ

A mansion in Brussels. A Hong Kong brothel. A hovel in Melbourne, and a second-floor walk-up flat not far from Buckingham Palace. The killer must have lingered in England after that one, because the next murder had taken place in a small town in the English midlands. He'd killed a young Russian aristocrat aboard a houseboat along the Volga River outside Kazan, and a sheep shearer in a little-known town in the Australian outback.

"Here. Look at this."

Local Beauty Slaughtered: Newcomer Suspected. Julie skimmed the front-page article in the *Tri-County Journal*, a tabloid weekly that apparently served three eastern Montana counties. The account, folksy in the style in which it was written, mirrored the articles she'd seen before. A grainy photo showed the victim before the tragedy, when she'd been crowned queen of the local rodeo a few months before her death.

"Alexandre caught up with Reynard here, shortly after he'd killed this dude rancher's daughter," Stefan whispered, passing Julie the next article. "Alex nearly got himself tried for murder by trying to enlist the help of that Montana sheriff. The trouble there held him up long enough that he and Claude arrived too late in Singapore to stop the next killing."

He'd mentioned that earlier, Julie remembered. Her doubts faded with every new piece of evidence they found in the newspaper archives. With each account, she found it easier to believe Louis Reynard might be a serial killer.

He'd slaughtered an Argentine beauty queen in a luxury hotel room in Buenos Aires. And just last week, a woman had been found in a run-down tenement near downtown Atlanta, her throat slit like all the rest. The woman Stefan had described in vivid, stomach-curdling detail. "I arrived moments too late to save her," Stefan said when he showed her the newspaper article about her death. "We fought, and I thought I had him. To my shame, I let him escape."

Reaching up, Julie traced the angry laceration on his cheek. Twenty women had died in all manner of places. They'd lived in varied circumstances, come from all walks of life. They'd all been tall, slender blondes and they'd died in the same horrific manner. "Is that how you got this?"

"Yes." He took her hand, brought it to his lips. "It's practically healed now."

Each newspaper report Julie saw made her grow sicker...more terrified. She looked at the chilling accounts of women dying, reported in English and Spanish and French and Russian, and other languages neither she nor Stefan could translate. Murder victims depicted in stark black and white photography needed no translation, though. Twenty women who looked eerily like her had been found naked and very, very dead, their throats slashed. Of the accounts they'd been able to read, none indicated the victims had been sexually assaulted, although from the newspaper accounts, they'd put up varying degrees of resistance to their killer.

It was all too terrifying to believe, yet the pattern was too clear to dismiss as coincidence. The work of a killer vampire. Or vampires. Julie tamped down on her fear. After all, how many of their numbers roamed the earth? Julie pictured that vase of white roses on the table in her townhouse, shuddered, then made a mental note to call the florist and learn for certain who had placed the order.

She didn't have to do it. Not really. Stefan had convinced her Louis Reynard was the serial killer. A killer who'd singled her out to become his next victim.

Suddenly it hit her. The next gory newspaper write-up might be about her. Would almost certainly be if they didn't do something quickly to thwart the bloodthirsty creature who almost certainly had sent her those roses.

Julie grasped Stefan's hand, spoke softly so other library patrons wouldn't overhear her. "What if I took copies of these articles to the police, told him you've been chasing this killer for months and pointed Mr. Reynard out so they could keep an eye on him? Surely they'd listen."

Stefan shook his head. "Just how would you link these murders to Reynard? They're not likely to accept the signature of the rose or to give credence to the latest note Reynard sent Alina. They've paid our reports no attention in the past. No, Julie, as much as we might like it otherwise, our only chance to defeat Reynard is to stick together and stop him when he makes his move."

When they walked out of the library, Julie thought Stefan looked drawn, tired. "I'm hungry. Shall we stop and get a bite to eat?"

Stefan took her hand, brought it to his lips. "You wouldn't happen to know where there might be a vampire bar or blood bank, now would you?"

"A vampire bar?" She'd heard whispers of such places on Rush Street but shrugged them off as the fanciful imaginings of mortals who embraced the Goth lifestyle. "Not really. Well, every hospital has a blood bank, but I doubt they'd sell blood for human—or vampire—consumption. As far as vampire bars go, I never accepted until this morning that vampires existed outside books and movies. Do many humans know about...people like you?"

"More than you'd expect." He cocked his arrogant brow, grinned. "Vampire bars can be found in most major cities if one knows where to look. The mortals who know about them are typically on the fringes of society, into alternative lifestyles, fetishes. They tend to be more accepting of...the unusual."

"Like a tattoo and body piercing shop owner, maybe?"

"It's possible. Do you know such a mortal?"

"I have a friend who owns that kind of shop. I do art designs for him. He's...somewhat like the type of person you described." She recalled some of Giorgio's tattoo designs, one in particular of a fearsome-looking vampire with blood dripping from his fangs. "What do you think? Is it worth a try?"

Stefan looked down at her, and his expression brought a flush to her cheeks. "You're an extraordinary woman, Julie, for believing me. Trusting me. Being willing to help me sustain myself for the fight ahead. Yes, let's give it a try."

She nodded, tightened a hand on his, and a grip on her fear. "Let's go then. If I get my own personal vampire bodyguard, I want him to be in top form." She slanted him a half smile. "If not, I'll cut your benefits."

Stefan's grin came slow and oh, so very sexy. "I'd like to see you try, *chèrie*. I'd like to see you try."

* * * * *

Shiny black and white and chrome accented with red Chinese symbols gave an upscale retro look to the tattoo and piercing salon. The sound of dishes clattering downstairs at the sushi bar clashed with soft classical music piped in through speakers mounted near the ceiling in all four corners of the reception room, where a receptionist had indicated they should wait.

"Giorgio is doing a piercing, Julie. He should be finished in a little while," she said before disappearing, apparently to tell her employer he had guests.

"Thanks, Mary." Julie squeezed Stefan's hand. "Come over here and let me show you some of Giorgio's work."

Stefan let her lead him past the black and white photos that adorned one wall. Apparently, he deduced, they were of Giorgio's piercings, noses and tongues and — he shuddered — genital piercings the likes of which he'd never before imagined. The opposite wall featured pen and ink drawings of intricate tattoo designs, including a couple that depicted fearsome-looking vampires with bloodshot eyes, their mouths curled into snarls, huge fangs dripping blood. One sported a high-collared black cloak lined in red, the epitome of Hollywood cliché. Stefan grimaced when he noticed the half-closed coffin in which the other vampire was ensconced. "Yours?" he asked.

"I drew some of them. Not the vampire ones, though."

He shot an arch look her way. "Now I know where you got your mental image of vampires."

"Not really. I never looked closely at these designs before." Julie stepped closer to the wall, pointed at one. "That one looks like the actor who played Dracula in all those old horror movies they play on late-night television. The ones Christopher Lee starred in."

Stefan recognized the actor. He and Alex had spent several pleasant evenings laughing over Lee's portrayals of Vlad Dracul. "Movies like that give us vampires a bad name."

He'd seen as much as he wanted to see of the tattoo artist's renditions of his kind. His hand on Julie's hip, he guided her further along the display wall, stopping to examine some designs that inspired awe, not horror. "I like these much better."

"So do I. I'm afraid the ones we just looked at are meant to appeal more to people who like tattoos for shock, not for their artistic value."

"Which ones are yours?" he asked, amazed at the fine detail evident in the designs.

Julie gestured toward an elaborate Maltese cross near the center of the display. "I created this one. One of Giorgio's clients wanted something different from the stock designs, yet nothing too outrageous. Giorgio's own original designs, like the ones of the vampires, were more elaborate than what the woman wanted to wear on her forearm."

The cross, in stained-glass colors that reminded Stefan of a window in a church not too far from his home, was breathtaking in its beauty and simplicity. He imagined running his fingers over the design once it was etched onto a woman's skin, experiencing silky living flesh beneath the muted jewel tones. "It's beautiful. Like you."

Julie laughed, a nervous sound. "I'm afraid I have a strong dislike of needles. Giorgio has never been able to persuade me to let him use me as a canvas for his art."

"One of my cousins once tried to get a tattoo. Apparently they don't work well on vampires. Though I assume we could become candidates for your friend's other specialty." Stefan glanced at the photos depicting jewelry on various body parts, most of which he preferred to keep private. "Not that I have an overwhelming desire to have metal stuck through my flesh."

"Neither do I. Come on, let's sit and relax. Giorgio takes his time when he's doing a new piercing."

An array of body jewelry lay in display cases built into the tops of lacquered tables someone had grouped artfully between black leather and chrome sofas and love seats. The heavy silver rings brought to mind his last meal, and the similar adornment he'd felt in his victim's cock. "Hmmm," he said, his attention drawn to some smaller pieces. "Those look suspiciously like cufflinks."

"I thought that too when I first saw them, but Giorgio said they're navel rings."

"Ah, yes. Like the harem dancers wear." A large round sapphire winked up at Stefan, making him wonder how it would look on Julie. "Have you ever…"

"No. As I said before, I'm afraid of needles. The only parts of me that I've had pierced are these." She tossed back her pale curls, calling his attention not only to the inviting column of her throat but to the small diamonds that pierced the lobes of her delicate, beautifully shaped ears. "I thought about doing my navel, but Giorgio says it's one of the most difficult piercings to heal. Basically, I'm a coward."

"Yes, you are." A little man, shorter than Julie and naked but for gym shorts and a body covered with tattoos, beamed at them when he emerged from a treatment room. His seemingly satisfied customer kept looking in every mirror, apparently admiring a fresh piercing through his lower lip. "Don't tell me you've brought me a new client," he said to Julie, giving her a big hug.

"No, Giorgio. This is my friend Stefan. Stefan, Giorgio Campione."

Stefan found Giorgio's handshake amazingly strong for one so small. "My pleasure," he said. "You do some interesting work." It was damn hard not to stare, for nearly every visible centimeter of Giorgio's body bore intricate, interwoven designs—and chains. A lot of flashy gold chains, one connecting a nostril with an eyebrow, another dangling from a loop pierced into the top of his ear and connected to the large hoop earring in his earlobe. Stefan couldn't help wondering. Could the heavy chain that ran through his nipple rings and disappeared into his shorts be hooked to a ring pierced through the man's cock, and if so didn't that have to be painful?

"The body's a perfect canvas, I keep telling Julie. She won't even trust me to give her a tiny rosebud tattoo where no one but a lover would ever see it." Giorgio sat down across from them and met Stefan's gaze. "What can I do for you, if not a decoration for your body or the pretty lady's? Your lady's?"

Julie's cheeks flushed when Giorgio winked at her with one of his too-shrewd eyes. Stefan hesitated a moment then met the mortal's questioning gaze. "You can point me in the direction of the nearest vampire bar."

"Should've known. You all have great skin. Would be fabulous to show off my most intricate designs, if only it had a bit more moisture…and elasticity. Still, I've had good luck with piercing vamps—you have remarkable healing abilities." Giorgio stood, unabashedly examining the laceration on Stefan's cheek. "Except for this. You'll be lucky if it doesn't leave a scar."

"It's a vampire bite. The venomous kind. We're susceptible to the poison, as much as any mortal. Would you know of a place around here where I can feed?"

"*Ristorante della Rubio,* over on Wilding Street, just off Rush. Ask for the manager. His name is Gus. Tell him in Italian that I said he could provide special refreshments for vampires. You do speak Italian, don't you?"

"Enough to ask a simple question." It didn't surprise him that this Gus took the precaution of screening its customers. Proprietors of vampire bars couldn't be too careful about who they admitted. "I assume the *Ristorante della Rubio* is a suitable place to take a lady."

"My vampire clients tell me they always stop in there whenever they're in the neighborhood." Giorgio glanced over at Julie. "You know you promised to paint me someday, so keep that in mind if you're thinking of running off with your handsome friend here."

Julie smiled. "It will take you months yet to finish tattooing your entire body. You told me you didn't want to pose until then."

"I finished. Want to see?" Giorgio slid his thumbs into the elastic waistband of his shorts.

"No thanks," Stefan said hastily, putting a firm hand under Julie's elbow and propelling her to her feet. The man was nearly enough naked already to make Stefan want to rip off his sweater and toss it over Giorgio's exposed flesh. He didn't need to see whether Giorgio had tattooed and pierced his cock and balls to match the rest of his short, stocky body, and neither did Julie. "Thanks for the information. I owe you."

But not enough to let you show off your body art to my woman.

Yes, Julie was his and his alone, until the danger from Reynard was past and Stefan had to walk away and leave her to live her mortal life. He relished the connection as well as the warmth of her fingers when she curled them around his palm, tried not to dwell on the sorrow of their imminent parting. "Shall we check out this *Ristorante della Rubio*?"

* * * * *

A few minutes later, when they stepped inside the posh entry foyer of the restaurant Giorgio had named, Julie saw a place not unlike every other establishment in the neighborhood. Well-dressed diners enjoyed wine from an impressive cellar while ordering from leather-bound menus she imagined bore steep prices—if any at all. Subtly sensual music flowed around them, the sounds muted so as not to interfere with intimate conversation. When Stefan asked for Gus, a hostess scurried off to find him, apparently unsurprised at the request.

A small, dark-haired man in a tuxedo strode toward them, a broad smile on his round, pleasant face. "Gus Rubio at your service. How may I help you today, my friends?"

"Giorgio ce li dice serv refreshments speciali per i vampires."

Though her Italian was rusty, Julie was pretty sure Stefan said Giorgio had mentioned the place served special refreshments for vampires. Feeling very much out of place and more than a little afraid, she laid her hand on Stefan's muscular forearm, concentrating on the conversation to translate as much as she could of the rapid Italian they spoke. From what she managed to decipher, she knew Stefan had introduced himself and identified his clan, and that Gus had shown great pleasure in meeting what he apparently considered an important guest.

Si. Segualo, i miei amici. Good. Gus had declared them friends and asked them to follow him somewhere. He lowered his voice, speaking now in unaccented English. "Come this way. I have a table for you among our very special guests."

Gus escorted them through the public rooms, leading the way through a swinging door to what she assumed led to the establishment's kitchen. It wasn't that at all, but a second lounge, just as luxuriously appointed, similar to the public area. Soft blues music wafted through the room from ceiling-mounted speakers, sensual sounds that surrounded and encompassed them. Muted strobe lights bathed the room in tones of red, purple, blue and green. A few couples swayed on a raised hardwood dance floor while others sat at small round tables or in darkened corner booths, apparently intent on enjoying their drinks and engaging in quiet conversation.

"Vampires?" All of the occupants looked perfectly normal to Julie, rather like an assortment of prosperous businesspeople out for a night on the town. Not a single one had blood-red lips, white-white skin, long red talons or a widow's peak. Not all of them even sported the raven-hued locks she'd associated with vampires even since she'd accepted Stefan's tale.

"Every one of them, except for a few mortal companions like you, miss." Gus smiled broadly, revealing his own needle-sharp fangs as he shifted his gaze to Stefan. "It's a real honor to have one of the d'Argent clan visiting with us. You just let us know if you or the pretty lady need anything."

"I imagine Julie would like a more conventional drink than what you serve back here." Stefan squeezed her hand. "Julie?"

This was too much. Not at all the dark, scary place she'd imagined. Her gaze traveled over the patrons again, men in business suits or casual attire, well-heeled women in their Donna Karan and Valentino creations. Except for an occasional flash of fangs and the universally dark-red color of the drinks they sipped with the same polite restraint as Julie had been taught to consume her own libations, the patrons looked much like those who'd been enjoying the cocktail hour in the main room she and Stefan had just passed through.

The past few hours had broadened her mind on the subject of vampires far more than she would have imagined. Every minute she was finding it easier to accept what Stefan had explained—that there were good and bad vampires, the same as there were good and bad mortals. It made her proud and happy to realize she was standing next to one of the good ones.

"Julie?" Stefan repeated her name, giving her hand a small squeeze.

"Oh. I'm sorry. I'll have a glass of red burgundy if it's not too much trouble." At least her drink would fit in, color-wise, with what seemed to be the other patrons' drink of choice.

Gus nodded. "We just got in a shipment of some fine vintages from the *Côte de Nuits* region. Fine, full-bodied reds. Perfectly matured to provide a silky-smooth taste. An exceptional quality wine, or so I'm told."

"The *Côte de Nuits* produces some of the most exceptional wines in Burgundy. Julie?" When she nodded, Stefan turned to Gus. "That will be fine. I'll have a large draft of O negative." Stefan rested his hand along the upper curve of Julie's buttock then glanced around the lounge. "You haven't seen any members of the Reynard clan lately, have you?"

"No, I haven't. I'm not likely to either. The Reynards aren't welcome in my club. Vicious, the lot of them, throwbacks to times no rational vampire would want to relive. They give law-abiding folks of our kind a bad name, every last one of them. You two relax, enjoy the music. I'll have a waiter bring your drinks."

Folks of our kind. Stefan's kind, but not Julie's. A frisson of fear—no, not fear but definitely unease—niggled at Julie's mind. She'd gotten caught up in the magic of Stefan's smile, the heady pleasure of his embrace. The carnal touch of some strange breed of creature, human yet not human, immortal. And she didn't really know the man—the vampire—to whom she'd offered her body, her trust. Though he'd told her where he lived, he'd omitted many of the most basic, immaterial details of his existence. Now that she was getting over the initial shock of learning what he was, she wanted more. More knowledge and more of him. "How old are you?" she blurted, meeting his glittering emerald gaze.

"Chronologically, a little over four hundred fifty years. The equivalent of around thirty in mortal years. Over the years, the older males of our clan have been destroyed, so I'm among the oldest hunters of my clan—yet a mere youngster compared with Reynard and many like him." He picked up the frosted mug a waiter had set before him and took a tentative sip of the dark-red fluid it held. "Not quite the quality I've come to expect in Paris, but it's good. Refreshing."

Julie couldn't help shuddering. Not so much at the sight of Stefan sipping blood from a mug, or even by the fact he'd just told her he'd lived for over four centuries, but at a woman on the dance floor who'd just sunk her teeth — fangs — into the neck of her partner. The look on the man's face hinted not at agony, but more like ecstasy. He looked almost as though he were experiencing a sexual climax right there on the floor. When he lowered his hands and cupped his partner's buttocks, Julie squirmed.

The woman's skirt swirled about his pale fingers, the burgundy chiffon dark — bloodlike — against his slacks. Soft, sensual, it moved with the breeze from their motion, kissing his dark gray suit pants and then retreating. They swayed to the escalating rhythm of muted drums and mellow woodwinds that spoke of smoke-filled rooms, a time live with action...untold forbidden pleasures.

I'm not a voyeur. I'm not. Yet Julie couldn't take her gaze away from the couple. She imagined the man dragging his partner to the floor, spreading her legs, returning her love-bite with many of his own. Not just on the pale column of her throat but on her nipples. Her belly. The insides of her quivering thighs. When he'd worked her into a frenzy of wanting, he'd tear away her panties, free his cock and fuck her right on the dance floor, oblivious to the stares — the yearnings — of their fellow customers.

Julie trembled with fear — and yearning too. What was it about this scene — highly erotic yet anything but pornographic — that made her yearn to drag Stefan onto the dance floor? To beg him to fuck her here and now? She met his gaze, saw raw hunger in his expression.

"That's the sort of a mating dance that made vampires enjoy. The males are unable to have conventional sex," Stefan explained, as though he'd read her mind.

Damn. She'd forgotten he was a telepath. He probably had been reading her every thought. She couldn't help remembering how he'd taken her last night. How he'd fit his huge, hard cock into her pussy and fucked her until she exploded in a blaze of sensation. Until he filled her with his come. Twice. "I remember now. You said you were—"

"A born vampire." He smiled, his fangs a flash of white made brighter by the colored lights. "Born vampires can mate as humans do. Occasionally we even produce a baby vampire to proliferate our clans.

"And yes, it would heighten your orgasm if I did to you what she's doing to him, at the moment I began to spill my seed. But I wouldn't. Couldn't. I'd risk turning you...or even killing you if I couldn't control my bloodlust."

"Turning me?"

"Making you like them. Consigning you to an eternity in my world."

Julie sipped her wine, savoring the rich, slightly fruity flavor of the fine vintage. Questions tumbled around in her mind, demanding to be set free, explored.

The otherworldly lovers' searing passion encompassed Julie like a soft, sensual cloak of fire, red, orange and electric blue. Erotic echoes of the mellow music caressed her ears, her soul. Her nipples tingled, and she grew damp between her legs. The dry, fruity essence of the fine red wine heated her throat, curled lovingly in her belly.

What was happening to her? She didn't get swept away by colors—by passion. The masters who'd tried to unleash her inhibitions and encourage her to express her feelings unabashedly in her art had given up, certain she lacked the emotional depth necessary for greatness.

Here in a den of vampires, though, the haze of convention that had dulled her emotions fled. She felt raw terror, not for her life but for her very being. Fear that was deep and real yet eclipsed by an insatiable desire to become part of the milieu, to immerse herself completely in her vampire lover. Excitement crackled all around her, and when she reached over and took Stefan's hand she experienced a jolt of carnal need, yet something more. A forever kind of feeling, a need for him to take her to that plane of ecstasy she sensed lay just beyond her grasp. "Dance with me," she whispered, every cell in her body aching for…

A taste of the rich, red fluid from his lips. Confirmation he was indeed of another time, another place, another world where he might take her, keep her cocooned in his desire so her own might flourish. A place where he would keep her safe from harm. Safe from the monster that was Louis Reynard.

"You don't know what you're asking of me." Setting down his mug, Stefan rose as though resigned to honor her plea, as tall, commanding a presence among his own kind as he was among Julie's. He held her chair then took her hand. A familiar song from Chicago's gangster era blared through the speakers, its heavy percussion and wailing woodwinds beating out a rhythm that brought to mind crowded dance halls, gun-toting molls, and hot, sweaty sex. When they stepped onto the hardwood dance floor, the strobe lights reflected brilliant shards of red and gold off his raven hair, forming a macabre halo that encompassed him and her in a kaleidoscope of sensation.

When he pulled her into the circle of his embrace, Julie knew. She wanted him. But did she want to say goodbye to her mortal existence, live for centuries by his side in a shadow world instead of decades as a mortal in the only world she knew? Watch generation after generation of her friends and loved ones age and die while she lived on? Could she bear living for centuries with her father no longer there to give advice and love?

You'd have centuries with Stefan. Forever in the safe haven of his embrace. Forever seeing all the shapes and colors in vivid hues, experiencing all the sensual, sexual pleasures of belonging to your vampire lover… Seduced by this place, the music, the seething sexuality he wrapped around her even as they swayed together fully clothed, Julie had her answer. She might regret it later, but she couldn't resist. It felt right. So right…

"I want it all. Bite me, Stefan. Transport me to a plane beyond anywhere I've ever been. Invade my heart and body and mind and make them yours."

He growled, a deep, anguished rumble that seemed to have come straight from his soul, but he grasped her hips, drew her close enough to feel the strength of his erection. Closer. The heat of his big hands molding the curve of her buttocks, the gentle motion of his breath on her hair, the brush of his chest against her nipples as he led her in the dance all stoked her desire to a fever pitch.

Then he took her mouth, wiped away any doubt that it was blood he'd drunk from that chilled stein. The slightly metallic taste was unmistakable, like the taste of her own blood when she'd sucked away the pain from a minor paper cut. Arousing, though, not revolting as she'd thought it might be. Hungry, she traced the seam of his lips with her tongue, blatantly inviting him to plunge inside. His groan of acquiescence tickled her lips, and she opened them to his tongue's insistent, rhythmic invasion.

God, but she wanted it all. Wanted it right here and now. Wanted him to raise her skirt, rip away her flimsy panties and impale her on his huge, rigid sex. She laid her head back, bared her throat as she'd seen the vampires do. "Bite me, now."

"You're just experiencing a dose of vampire sexual attraction," he said, a touch of desperation in his voice. "Vampires have a strong seductive effect on mortals. I used it that first night to get you to let me into your home."

"Are you using it now?"

"No, but—"

"Did you use it to seduce me?"

"Julie," he said, his voice ragged. "No. Of course not. But-"

"Then my feelings are my own. Nothing you've planted in my mind. They're only for you, no one else in this room." She paused then looked into his eyes. "Did you want me, or was it all a trick?"

"I wanted you."

"Then want me now."

Maybe it was the atmosphere, or the influence of the otherworldly people around them, because Julie almost didn't care that he'd influenced her that first night to save her life, and maybe other times he hadn't told her about. She didn't even care if he'd used his vampire powers to get her into bed. She knew he wanted her, as a woman always knew. That was all that mattered.

Though her masters had despaired of her artistic abilities, Stefan had somehow unleashed the depths of her emotions by his compelling presence. She recalled Giorgio's once having insisted she was a true artist, and as such she had the ability to see beyond the surface. Perhaps she did, for now her inhibitions fled. She saw truth, uncolored by doubt or fear. Stefan was trying to protect her, but her true protection lay here, as close to him as she could get. "I want it all," she whispered again.

He drew her closer, so close the pulsating heat of his hard, throbbing cock seared her belly. His ragged breathing beat a staccato path along her temple...her jaw...her throat. She held her breath, waiting, but he came no closer. Instead he looked down into her eyes, his expression tortured. "I cannot. Cease tempting me, Julie, for I must not do this."

She tried to talk, to persuade him he must, but the only sound that escaped her was a pitiful whimper...and a sob.

"It's for the best. Come, I'll get some carryout and take you home."

Chapter Eight

ॐ

Stefan had never been so hard, so ready. Instead of beating slowly as it usually did, his heart pounded in his chest, pumping blood furiously through his tortured body. His fangs ached. Julie trembled beside him, her arousal obvious by the desperate way she clasped his thigh, the unmistakable scent of female musk that filled his nostrils. If the distance to her townhouse had been even a kilometer longer, he'd have been unbearably tempted to lift her onto his lap, tear away the flimsy barrier of her panties and fuck her then and there.

When they arrived, she handed him her key, her hand shaking. "You do it. I can't."

He shifted one of the rice cartons that contained his meals for the next few days to the other hand, took the key, and opened the door. "Do you have somewhere I can keep this cold?"

"This way." Her motion jerky, as if she was in a hurry, she led the way to the kitchen and opened the refrigerator door. "In here," she said before turning to let Noodles in from the patio. "Hey, girl. It's your bedtime."

The refrigerator lit the otherwise darkened room, showcasing its contents—milk, eggs, some dainty-looking plastic cups of yogurt with pictures of fat black cherries and ruby-colored raspberries. A ripe peach and a slice of strawberry cheesecake. The neatly arranged food underscored the fact they were from different worlds. Stefan set the cartons on an empty shelf then closed the door with a hard thud.

The wall between them shouldn't be breached. She'd lose too much. The tastes of Earth's bounty. The warmth of the noonday sun. Sounds and smells and touches so familiar to mortals, so alien to those of his kind who thrived in darkness. That barrier must not be breached, no matter how much they might both wish it otherwise.

He could not change for her. She must not change for him. The passion that sizzled between them could not, must not last other than in his memories. With the room now in total darkness, he took her hand and led her, for she had not his ability to see in the dark, to the room where they'd first made love.

Yes, they'd made love. Not merely fucked to slake their mutual lust. Because he loved her, he'd meet her needs once more…take her to the heights of passion and beyond. But he wouldn't change her. He'd save her from himself even if doing so destroyed him, and then he'd walk away. Even though he sensed that leaving her would do more to harm him than Louis Reynard ever could.

Maybe… Stefan considered how easily Claude had turned his mortal mate just weeks ago. How happy Marisa seemed to be, living in their vampire world. No. The centuries-old memory of Tina lying dead, victim of his love, flooded Stefan's mind, steeled his resolve.

Beside her bed, he gently removed Julie's clothes and his own. Her little whimpers when he stroked her fed his need, but also steeled his determination to save her from himself as well as the Fox. He concentrated on bringing her desire slowly back to fever pitch, while holding his own desperate need ruthlessly in check.

Her pale hair felt like silk between his fingers, looked like spun gold in the dim light of the moon. He tunneled his fingers among the strands, indulging his need to taste her by claiming her mouth. With heart-wrenching trust he swore would not prove misplaced, she opened to him, welcomed his tongue's thrusts and met them eagerly. Her tongue tangled with his, brushed against the tips of his fangs, tempting him almost beyond his ability to resist. The heat of her hands on his bare back and ass felt so good. So right. As though fate had meant this to be. Meant her to be his mate.

Stefan deepened the kiss, anticipating... She'd taste sweet, so much sweeter than his sustenance. Like nectar, not necessity. He'd pierce her lightly, take just a sip.

You must not.

Giving heed to his inner voice, he broke the kiss, foiled temptation for now. Groaning audibly, he swept both hands down her body, cupping her beautiful breasts, rubbing his fingers gently over already engorged nipples and kneading the warm, pale flesh. "You like that, don't you?" he asked when she moaned with apparent pleasure.

"I love the feel of your hands on me. Love tasting you." When she bit into his shoulder with her benign human teeth, it was all he could do not to retaliate, sample all she'd so clearly offered, all he must not accept. "I love the way your skin feels so smooth beneath my hands and lets me trace each muscle beneath its satin surface."

When she moved her fingers along his pectoral muscles and found the sensitive flesh of his own nipples, he suddenly had to breathe. When he inhaled deeply, the mingled scents of her perfume and aroused mortal female filled his nostrils. The touch of her fingers on his belly, the little sounds of pleasure she made when he touched her—when she touched him—had his balls growing tighter, his cock throbbing harder than he recalled ever having experienced before.

Being with her in his world, the world of night, seeing her silhouetted by the waning moon, her golden skin and pale hair absorbing the little light and giving her a surrealistic glow, made him want so much more than he dared to take. He wanted to invade her mind and heart, make her his not just for now. For always. Stefan had never been so hard, so ready—or so afraid he might lose control.

If he took her...he could destroy her.

She cupped his sex and tilted her head back to meet his gaze. "Make love to me now, my handsome vampire. Take away the ache inside me. Now, Stefan. I'm burning."

More than her words, the breathy, highly aroused sound of her voice drove him past reason, past restraint. The pulsating vein in her throat caught his gaze, taunted him. It was all he could do to control himself, hold his fangs back when they wanted so to elongate, to answer her blatant invitation with the act that might make her eternally his—or destroy her forever.

"Do not tempt me. I will make love to you in your world, but I cannot take you into mine." Scooping her into his arms as though she weighed no more than Noodles, he laid her across the bed and followed her down, kneeling between her widespread legs. Her damp heat reflected on him, beckoned him.

"Oh yes, please. Don't wait. I want you now."

"Your wish is my command." When he positioned himself and started to enter her, she wrapped her long legs around his waist, sucking him in deep, bathing his cock in her hot, slick dew. Her hot, swollen cunt pulsated around him in perfect harmony with the thrumming of blood through his veins. She moved in perfect rhythm with him, thrust and retreat. So deep. It felt so right. Pressure built in his cock, his balls, throughout his body. Driving away caution, restraint. Robbing him of the fragile strands of sanity he was trying so hard to hold onto.

She lay across the bed, her head slightly over one side, her throat bared, taunting him again with that throbbing vein just below her golden skin. Stefan closed his eyes, trying to put that enticing vision out of mind. He concentrated on the way her tight cunt felt when she used her inner muscles to milk his cock, the rush of pressure building in his balls. The tickling of her silky pubic hair against his smooth scrotum. She pulled him down on her with her legs until they lay chest to breast, belly to belly. Until his cock was buried to the hilt in her silken heat, his balls bathed with her hot wet juices.

"Stefan. Oh God, I'm coming." Her climax began as tiny tremors, multiplied and intensified until she writhed beneath him, whimpering his name. Moaning, digging her heels into his ass, she clutched him as though she'd never let him go. She shifted her hands to his head, drew him down against her vulnerable throat. Her vein pulsed invitingly beneath his cheek, so temptingly that he barely resisted her effort to move him into perfect alignment.

"Damn it, bite me. Don't hold back. I want it all. All you've got to give." She clamped down on his cock with her inner muscles, broke the last of his restraint.

"You don't know what you ask. I cannot. Help me, don't tempt me. I'm coming now." As his seed began to spurt, Stefan shoved his own forearm into his mouth, burying his fangs, tasting his own blood, letting his climax carry him away from the pain of denial…to a surprisingly satisfying place.

A place where differences between them didn't matter. Where good always triumphed over evil.

Chapter Nine

ﾥﾥ

She still lay beneath him. Her tears dampened his shoulder. Stefan pressed his nose into her hair, wishing he didn't have to raise his head and see the hurt in her eyes. He knew it was there, felt it in every rigid line of her beautiful body. "I'm sorry."

Knowing he'd disappointed Julie caused Stefan greater pain than the throbbing puncture wounds he'd made in his own arm. He rolled over, blocking the view of the rising sun by covering his eyes. "We need to talk. I need to tell you—"

"I have to take Noodles for a walk." She sounded miffed but calm.

Stefan raked a hand through his hair, wishing it would help his headache go away. He started to curl his hand around her arm, keep her stubborn, lovely ass on that bed until he made her listen. But that wasn't how he wanted to handle her. She needed a moment, needed space. Hell, he needed some himself. "Fine. But I'm going with you. It's not safe for you to go out alone, especially now when it's hardly even light outside."

Sitting up on the edge of the bed, he reached on the floor and grabbed his clothes. "Wait. I'm getting dressed. You are not going anywhere unless I go with you."

"I don't need a babysitter, Stefan. You said yourself that Louis would try to strike in two more nights. Not now. And not in the daytime."

Stefan pulled up his slacks and slipped his feet into his loafers. Then he stood. "Indulge me. Reynard has already modified his pattern of killings. He might do it again. He might very well be waiting for you in the park, assuming that you'll be walking Noodles. Are you ready?"

"Yes."

"Let's go, then." He picked up the dog's leash and handed it to Julie.

The sun rising over Lake Michigan practically blinded Stefan when they stepped outside. Mentally cursing his weakness, he slipped on the dark glasses. Hated them. Hated that they suddenly represented all the reasons he couldn't take Julie, make her his own.

This was her world. A world where she could exchange pleasantries with an elderly couple like this one they passed not far from Julie's house. A world where he had to take care not to show his fangs and hope the couple's fragile Yorkie on its braided satin leash wouldn't sense danger and dig its razor-sharp teeth into his ankle.

"I'm happy to meet you," he said with a careful smile, vaguely aware Julie had introduced him as her friend from Normandy. Because the old woman seemed to expect it, he bent and brought her thin hand to his lips after shaking hands with her husband. Fortunately the Yorkie seemed disinclined to bite him, although it didn't take to him the way Noodles had.

"I see them walking their dog every once in a while," Julie mentioned after they'd parted company. "They seem so loving, and they always have a kind word for everyone they see. Each time I see them, they seem less robust...I wonder..." She looked at him, as though she thought he might be the salvation of mortal mankind.

"No. If they were to become vampires, they'd be old, sick vampires. We have no ability to reverse aging or cure mortal ills."

"Oh. Then you only turn young, healthy mortals?"

"Julie. I don't turn mortals at all. No matter how much I might want to."

He hated the way her lower lip quivered, as though she wanted to cry but was determined not to. Feeling helpless, devoid of words to make things better, Stefan smiled hopefully at the couple coming toward them.

"A beautiful dog," he commented loudly enough that the owner of the elaborately clipped white miniature poodle would be certain to hear.

"Why, thank you." The poodle's owner, a statuesque black woman with a heavy accent, smiled broadly then bent to admire Noodles. Her sandy-haired companion, who reminded Stefan of the stereotypical all-American mortal male, grinned.

"Can't separate a woman from her dog, can we?" he asked, shaking his head. "At least you don't have to take that one to the groomer every Friday afternoon."

Stefan glanced down at Noodles then at the beribboned, perfumed poodle. "Every Friday?"

"Yep. If Princess misses her bath, Areatha says her coat begins to get dusty looking. How long can yours go?"

Stefan shrugged. "I'm not sure. Julie?"

"I bathe Noodles once a month. She's low maintenance." Julie looped her free arm through his, giving him the feeling that while he wasn't totally forgiven, she felt better for having gotten out and about in her world. "Speaking of maintenance, we'd better be going. Noodles is going to want her breakfast."

"I'm sure we'll see you again," the other woman told them as she tugged on her dog's hot-pink leash. "Take care."

"Those two are from different worlds, Stefan. She's cosmopolitan, elegant, obviously a world traveler. He's like a small-town boy from the way he speaks. It seems they've managed to bridge the gap." Julie interlaced their fingers once they'd moved along, then paused to look out and admire the sunrise. "Why can't we?"

Stefan let out an audible sigh. "They're both mortal. They occupy the same world, have the same expectations about who they are and the kind of life they'll lead together. Acceptance as members of the same species. We do not."

"You're here. You function just fine, from all I've been able to observe." She paused, raking him with a glance that was half teasing, half sexual—hopeful and serious all at once. "The only difference I see between us is that you get your nourishment from blood instead of conventional food. And, of course, the fact you're the most desirable male I've ever had the pleasure of loving."

He took her hand, led her to a bench under the shade of a large, spreading tree. "Could you stand living in darkness, rarely venturing out? Not seeing much of the beauty you now preserve in your art?"

She glanced at the bright sky then looked at him. "Sunlight has proven to be disastrous to a woman's skin. Besides—"

"As vampires age, they become less sensitive to light. You would be a very young vampire for a very long time. Perhaps as long as several mortal lifetimes. Another thing. I've seen how you enjoy your food. If you became like me, you not only would get your nourishment from blood, you probably would never be able to consume any other substance without becoming deathly ill."

"On the other hand, I'd still look and feel young when mortals my age would have long been dead. I'd get to love you for centuries, not decades, see our children—"

"That might not happen, no matter how diligently I'd try." He hated to burst her bubble but... "The reason there are so few born vampires is that we don't procreate easily. With luck, I might be able to father one child. I know of only one, my own grandfather, who managed to sire more—three sons over a period of nearly eight hundred years. Many of my clan have lived and died childless, not for want of trying."

"I don't care." She turned to him, laid one hand on his shoulder and the other on his thigh. "I know this doesn't make sense, Stefan. Don't you think I realize how crazy it is for me to feel this way? What is it that's made me feel so strongly about you in such a short time?"

When she smiled at him, Stefan couldn't help but smile back. "I don't know. You've given me the greatest pleasure I've known for centuries. Centuries, Julie. I cannot deny I want you for my own. But I'm a four-hundred-and-fifty-year-old vampire. You're a human. You flourish in the sunshine, while I move freely only in the shadows."

"But you're outside now. You were yesterday too. Why couldn't I—"

Stefan held up his hand to silence her. "You'd move even less freely than I. I may seem to move easily in the sunlight, but I've been a vampire all my life, and tolerance to the sun seems to increase as born vampires age. It doesn't mean being outside in the light is comfortable for me, even this early in the morning."

He paused, barely able even after all this time to put into words the fact of his youthful selfishness, his shame. The grief had faded, yet guilt still rode him hard. "I need you to understand...why. Why I can't take what I want more than anything."

"Then tell me. It won't make any difference about how I feel." Squaring her shoulders and grasping both his hands, Julie looked him in the eye, as though daring him to test her conviction.

"It will. It must. I loved a mortal once before. I wanted to keep her enough to try to turn her. She's dead. Because I loved her, I killed her. In my selfishness to keep her with me, I drained her lifeblood."

Julie drew in a breath, but as she searched his face with her gaze, she didn't recoil in horror. Her eyes filled with tears, as though registering the pain it had taken him to say the words. He loved her, more than he'd ever loved before, and she wasn't making this any easier. Her grip tightened on his fingers. "Don't try to tell me you ever hurt any woman intentionally. I may not have known you long, but I know you well enough to know that."

"No. But Tina was no less dead because I killed her out of love, not vengeance." Nearly two hundred years had passed, and still thinking about the lover of his youth made Stefan choke up, not so much with guilt as with regret for the youthful arrogance that had made him believe he could turn her into the vampire mate he'd yearned for.

"I'm sorry." When he looked into her eyes he saw no fear, no revulsion. Only sympathy…and love.

Emotions that made Stefan's own eyes well up with tears because he knew he'd have to walk away from Julie, knowing how deeply she cared, how much she trusted him despite his initial deception. His heart ached. Leaving her would hurt her, and hurting her would literally destroy him, end his existence long before his natural demise.

Or else he'd lose control and turn her, ending her life if he failed, changing it forever if he succeeded. He couldn't chance history repeating itself. "I won't consign you to living forever in darkness," he ground out, steeling himself against the power of her entreaties.

"I want you to." Her eyes glistened with ice-blue tears.

Stefan clasped her hands, compelled her to meet his gaze. "I won't risk killing you to feed my own obsession."

"How about for love? I'm not an obsession. You love me, damn it. I can see it in your eyes. I feel it in your touch."

Stefan closed his eyes. Since he couldn't guarantee he could bring her across to him safely, he wished he could change for her. If it were possible he'd shed the mantle of darkness and step into the light. Claim Julie. Raise a family with her, watch them grow up and have their own children. Their grandchildren. Not even the thought of dying young—having only fifty years or so to love his golden woman—dampened his sudden desire to leave his world. Become a part of hers.

It couldn't be, though. There would be no children, for he could only sire a child on another vampire, one born or one he'd made. "Yes. I love you. Too much to stay with you here, watch you ostracized by your friends. Too much to risk changing you in order for you to bear my child."

Julie's eyes widened, as if that thought hadn't crossed her mind before. "We've risked that already."

Stefan took her hand, stroked the soft skin, admired the pinkness of her short, neatly trimmed nails. "No, we haven't. No mortal can nurture a vampire's seed."

She choked back a sob. Her hands shook, revealing at last some of the emotional drain the past hour must have extorted from her.

"I'm sorry." He put his arms around her, offering comfort...shared regret...a mutual wish for what must not be. For what he must not allow to become, for her sake.

Noodles barked, her hackles rising on her long, round back. Stefan spun around on the bench, saw a flash of a white shirt and dark pants, an apparition swallowed almost instantly by the park's thick foliage behind them.

He pulled Julie to her feet, and she saw his eyes turn icy jade as he scanned the area in all directions. A moment earlier, he'd been pensive and sad, trying to persuade her she didn't know her own mind. Now he'd turned fierce. The tips of his fangs gleamed in the early sun, and he let out a low, menacing hiss—a hiss she recognized as a clear warning to any who dared threaten what was his. It froze her in his grasp, made her see him as a man who had gone from gentle nobleman to fierce predator in mere seconds. For her. To protect her.

This was the man she loved. The man she now understood would protect her, even at the cost of his own life. Even if that meant protecting her from dangers he himself posed to her safety. Dangers she must find a way of persuading him she'd face with joy, if only they might hope to share a lifetime together.

After a few tense moments, he loosened his painful grip on her arm. "Reynard," he spat out, the name projecting more hate than the most violent of curses. "He was here, spying on us. Come on, let's go home. For the time being, he's crawled back into his hole."

* * * * *

Louis huddled in the darkened cocoon of his hotel room, sealed off from daylight and danger. But sleep wouldn't come. He'd taken in stride the presence of one d'Argent shadow, even laughed at the young vampire's apparent inability to shield himself from view. But another? It seemed this one had taken to trailing not him but his next victim. Louis clenched his fists until the nails cut into his palms, his fury building by the moment as he pictured them together, Julie's bright head nestled on the broad shoulder of some wet-behind-the-ears youngster from the d'Argent clan.

Julie Quill was his. Only his, for all eternity, like all the rest. Not d'Argent's. Never his.

The d'Argent pup had been holding Julie as though he had the right. As though he knew her body as only mortals or born vampires could. Louis imagined d'Argent caressing her first, the way Louis had wanted to stroke Alina, nipping at her lips and throat and breasts before burying his face between her legs and sampling the honey there. Finally, when she was hot enough, he'd drive his male tool into her warm, moist human cunt and clamp down on her jugular to feed.

No. D'Argent hadn't turned the woman. Not yet. Louis would have sensed it if his victim had become a vampire. With jerky movements, for being outside in the dim light of dawn had burned away much of his strength, Louis straightened his legs and unclenched his right fist long enough to curl it around his useless prick.

It felt soft, malleable, cool. Once it had been hot and hard.

It had been the feast of the summer solstice, 1102. A mountain village in the Caucasus, a celebration of the series of successful raids that had filled each hut with food and drink. Much wine had flowed, so much that Louis had dared to rape the nubile daughter of a tribal chieftain in full view of all, including his own wife and the girl's sister and brothers. The chieftain had whacked off his balls then buried him alive in the small town cemetery.

Nine hundred years and more had passed since a vampire of the Reynard clan had plundered that village and taken refuge in the wooden coffin where Louis had lain. Louis still felt the fangs sinking into his neck, the slow return to consciousness, the agonizing pain in his groin from where the chieftain had castrated him several days earlier.

The ghoul who had restored his life had laughed when asked to give him back his stones. "They're of no use to the likes of us, my friend," he said. "I'm called Igor the Fox. Come with me. We'll wander the world in search of blood to drink. You're now a creature of the night…a vampire whose only pleasure will come from the taking of life from mortals."

Nine hundred years. Nearly a millennium since Louis had swelled with sexual energy. Too long.

For years he'd blamed Igor, wished the other vampire had let him rest in peace. He'd even rejoiced when his maker had been destroyed by a vampire hunter during the craze following the reign of Vlad Dracul. A lost soul, Louis had migrated with his clansmen, first to Prussia then to France, always seeking fulfillment that lay beyond his reach. Three useless brides. A string of dead humans on whom he'd fed had marked his path until he'd finally outlasted the others, ascending to leadership over his depleted clan two years ago.

One of the leader's supposed duties was to sire an heir, though none in his memory had ever accomplished that feat. Louis had gone to the eldest of his clan, a crone who'd been ancient when Igor had turned her centuries earlier, and sought her advice as to how best to make this miracle happen. She'd cackled and mocked him, told him what he asked was impossible, and so he'd tortured her. He'd broken her fragile bones and disemboweled her, yet refused to drive the wooden stake through her rotten heart and end her suffering until she told him what to do.

Her eyes had turned dark as death, their fire extinguished by pain, but she'd summoned up enough strength to hold his gaze and choke out a few clearly audible words. "Go…find the queen of the born vampires, the d'Argents. Join forces with her, and you'll be able to mate. Now, I beg you, grant me death, for the injuries you've inflicted on me will never heal."

Louis had believed her then and ended her suffering, certain she'd not have dared lie with her dying breath. He'd wondered, certainly, for the Reynard connection with the aristocratic d'Argent clan had been one of envy on the part of his clan, disdain on theirs. Over the centuries the d'Argents had blamed Reynards for the destruction of their elders — more often than not with justification. Still, Louis had trusted the vampire's last words, done as she'd bade him do.

Louis knew now. The bitch had lied. The more he'd hurt her, the more absurd lies she'd spun. Ha! The crone only thought she'd known pain. Pain he'd increase tenfold now if only he had the power to resurrect her from her grave.

He'd gone to Paris with such hope, such joy. Practically prostrated himself before the snobbish beauty who headed the d'Argent clan. She'd laughed. Laughed at him, Louis Reynard. Her minions had barely been able to repress the looks of disgust, of disbelief that he'd dared to suggest…

Alina had mocked him, tossed off his pitiful suggestion that they might join forces in governance if not in life. She'd live to regret that smile, that patronizing way she'd lifted one perfect eyebrow over one green d'Argent eye. Apparently the mere idea she'd sully her incomparable face and body on the likes of a Balkan-born peasant-turned-vampire had amused her.

So what if she'd known he personally had taken part in the series of vampire attacks that had brought disaster down on all vampires at the hands of the evil regent, Catherine de Medici. So she'd realized he'd had a hand in causing a bloody, painful death to her father and the elder one of her uncles. That was no fucking excuse for the bitch to have treated him, head of the Reynard clan, with such disrespect.

Louis doubted Alina was laughing now that she knew twenty women had died because of her cruelty, her mockery. He reached between his legs, felt his flaccid cock and the empty space his balls had filled when he was mortal. Fuck, he'd not only kill Julie Quill but destroy her d'Argent lover too.

"You'll soon see just what happens, Queen Alina," he muttered. "Nobody, not even the Queen of the Vampires, gets by with crossing the Fox."

First, though, Louis needed rest. Then a quick feed. To perdition with the moon cycles and the pattern he'd chosen to time his killings, creating a schedule of sorts that would keep Alina on edge, knowing when but not where he'd strike again. It was time now to alter his mode of operation, get his pursuers off balance. Keep taunting Alina as he'd vowed to do from the moment he'd walked out of her elegant Paris townhouse, ego battered but no more broken than his body had been when laid in that shallow grave so long ago. He'd sleep and feed, and then he'd confront the d'Argent whoreson in the arms of his mortal lover.

As he was drifting into that shadow world between wakefulness and sleep, Louis remembered the dog. While he was at it, he'd do in that damned sausage dog of hers that had dared to bite him — the same dog he'd seen again this morning, frolicking peacefully at d'Argent's feet.

* * * * *

Noodles laid her head on Stefan's foot while he sat with Julie, watching her prepare her breakfast. The bowl of plump, dark-red cherries and one creamy peeled banana let off an interesting fragrance — sweet-tart, in stark contrast to the slightly sulphur-like smell of the egg she was cooking on the stove.

"I hope that tastes better than it smells," Stefan commented when she scooped out the egg and set it on a slice of toast.

"It does." She set the plate on the table, then turned to the refrigerator and set out one of the carryout containers he'd brought home from the vampire bar. "Would you like a glass? Ice?"

"A small glass, please. No ice." Stefan had to give Julie credit. Not many mortals of his acquaintance would calmly have offered to let him feed while they ate their mortal fare. "I don't feed as often as I've observed that you mortals tend to eat, but I'll sip a bit while you have your breakfast."

If he hadn't been here, he imagined Julie would have pulled the shades open. The room would have reflected the bright outdoor light, patterned with the shapes of leaves and flowers from the plants she grew on the patio. As it was, the white walls reflected light, made it necessary for Stefan to keep on his dark glasses or risk contracting one awful headache. Still, this felt right, sitting in her kitchen, sipping his sustenance while she nibbled daintily on a juicy cherry.

When a rivulet of succulent-looking juices ran down her chin, Stefan had a sudden urge to taste it. Temptation, much like what he felt when he was a child playing in the vineyards near his home, overcame him. "The juice of the grape is sweet, but not for us," his mother used to say, her tone wistful. He'd dared taste the grape, suffered the bellyache, learned by doing so that mortal foods were not for him. Yet he leaned closer, stroked Julie's cheek, licked the sweet intoxicating juice away.

"Delicious. All the more so because it came from you." Stefan expected a vague, passing sense of nausea from the small, careful taste, but somehow he was not surprised when it didn't happen. It was as though his body knew and accepted this gift from his mortal lover, as if all the gods of vampires were looking down, approving their liaison.

She licked her lips where his had just touched her, smiled. Her eyes shone with passion, the way they did when they made love. Deliberately she reached on her plate, lifted the banana and brought it to her lips. "This doesn't taste as good as you."

His cock swelled as she sucked the sweet-smelling fruit, her gaze fixed on his face. Every swipe of her agile tongue, each delicate bit of pressure she exerted on the banana rushed through his body, had the same effect on his cock. "Is doing that making your pussy wet?" he asked in a rough whisper. He liked teasing her, sharing a simple, sensual moment free—for the moment—of more serious concerns.

"Mmm." Her nipples grew, hardened perceptibly beneath his gaze and her light cotton blouse. She drew her legs slightly apart as she slid the banana deeper into her mouth then withdrew it, only to slide it deeper yet. Stefan inhaled, savored the scent of her arousal that fed his own.

She drew the banana from her mouth, held it to his lips. "I can't," he said, though his mouth fell open to taste the moist, smooth sweetness of the forbidden fruit.

"Sorry." Setting the rest of the banana on the table, she sank onto her knees and loosened Stefan's belt. Noodles yelped, as though indignant that Julie had roused her from her resting place.

He'd worried that she'd find his body odd…repulsive because of its paleness, the lack of hair. Not to mention his fangs. She seemed to like all the things that made him different from her kind, and that kept his arousal at a fever pitch.

Stefan smoothed the curtain of blonde hair back from Julie's face, watched her rosy lips encircle his alabaster cock head, her delicate fingers cup his scrotum then stroke gently along his inner thighs. When she looked up at him, he saw lust…but more. He saw love. Love that filled him with awe—and helped him steel his resolve not to let go of his tightly held control.

The soft whisper of her breath tickled his belly when she sank lower on his swollen cock. Cooling, yet scorching a path along his body straight to his heart. Pressure built within his balls, tight, insistent.

Not this way. Not now. Lifting Julie from her spot between his legs, he slid up her skirt, reached for her panties…found warm, damp flesh instead. "I like it that you're already wet and ready. I'm going to fuck you now." He set her astride him, impaling her, sinking once more into her giving, heated cunt. Finding not just warmth…not only the prospect of release, but the promise of unconditional love.

The colors and sounds and smells of the world — of mortals — surrounded them. He grasped the lush flesh of her hips, lifted her almost free, only to slam her down again and again. She felt good. Tight yet giving. She took the full length of his cock into her body, cradling his balls between her swollen outer lips. Every welcoming squeeze of her wet, swollen cunt around his cock felt right. Perfect.

Stefan kept telling himself the feeling was only illusion born of long self-denial. As he held Julie's trembling body, absorbed her climax into his own, though, he knew this was different. This wasn't only sex. Not now. With every fiber of his being, he wanted to crawl into Julie's mind and stay. Merge their lives as well as their bodies. As his orgasm began, he realized the truth with every spurt of heated life into her womb.

He had to protect her from Reynard, but he yearned to claim her for himself.

* * * * *

Stefan had bathed, shaved and crawled into Julie's bed exhausted after they'd made love in the kitchen. Even after she'd drawn the drapes, the room seemed bright — too bright for her lover's sensitive eyes. Slipping out of bed, being careful not to wake him, she padded down the hall past the living room.

Suddenly the roses she'd thought so beautiful when the florist's son had delivered them made her stomach roil. The fragrance of the blossoms, now fully opened, overwhelmed her. Scooping them from their place on the table, she took them to the kitchen and fed them to the garbage disposal. Noodles barked as the disposal chewed the blossoms and stems, as though she understood and approved of what Julie was doing.

"I have to find something to block the light so Stefan can sleep," she said when Noodles trotted after her into the spare bedroom she used as a studio, sat on her haunches and looked up questioningly at her.

What she needed was something dark and big enough to drape across the French doors that faced her bed. Certain she'd find something, she began rifling through her supplies. No, blank canvases wouldn't do. Neither would the length of gossamer silk she first dragged from her stash of fabrics. It would let too much light through. There. She finally saw what she'd been looking for, folded neatly in the bottom of a large drawer. She fished out a large, dark-blue linen rectangle she'd bought to paint on and make an Indian sari. It would work perfectly to keep the sunlight at bay.

As she stuffed the other material back into the drawer, she decided she really ought not to buy any more until she used up all she had. More material than she could use in ten lifetimes, her father always said when he came to visit. Julie smiled at the thought of her dad, imagining how he'd react to Stefan.

Sam would like him. He'd approve of Stefan's protectiveness, his determination to take care of her. For a moment she shoved the truth of Stefan's resistance to letting them be together to a far corner of her mind. They'd travel to New Orleans, meet Sam in the French Quarter townhouse he'd restored and now used as the offices for his importing business.

Hugging the dark-blue length of linen to her breasts, she let her mind wander. Fantasized about a wedding at the Garden District home where she'd grown up. Her father would hand her over to Stefan while her friends and his looked on. Sensual sounds filled her ears, sounds of a blues band playing the mellow music she'd known and loved all her life. Guests would mingle as they dined on jambalaya and *etoufee*—and crystal tumblers of fresh blood. Not even the knowledge that so much of New Orleans had been decimated by Hurricane Katrina last year would dare intrude on her fantasy celebration.

Julie laughed. Before she planned her wedding, she must first persuade her lover she wanted him above all else. Beyond life as she knew it. Beyond mortal concerns like menus and seating arrangements and deciding upon the most flattering shade for her bridal veil.

Tidying the canvases where she'd rifled through them, she scooped up the linen, looped it over her arm and turned for the door. It was then her gaze fell on the huge canvas she'd stretched and primed earlier in the week, without a clue as to what she was going to do with it. Inspiration and emotion swelled in her, fueling a desire to create. Strange, but Stefan had had that effect on her almost since the moment they first met, of making her see things more clearly, feel them more deeply than before.

The canvas stood on its easel, buffed and sandpapered and waiting only for a subject to be portrayed. Now she had it. She'd paint Stefan. The most beautiful male specimen she'd ever seen. If he refused her pleas to take her, she could preserve him with her art.

He'd be hers forever on canvas, a frail reflection of the man — the vampire — she loved. She eyed the digital camera on the counter, but instead picked up a large sketchpad and a tray of colored pencils when she remembered that in the movies, vampires couldn't be captured on film. She'd sketch him on paper while he slept, record his image with her own hand instead of the camera's eye.

Chapter Ten

ප

Back in the bedroom, where sunbeams now filtered gently through her makeshift drape, Julie pulled up a chair and stared at Stefan's arresting features while her eyes grew accustomed to the muted light. The only flaw she noticed on casual observation of his face was the still angry-looking laceration that marred his left cheek. Louis Reynard's work. The man who'd already murdered twenty women and now wanted to kill her too.

While the horror of that thought shivered up her spine, Julie realized an even greater fear. God, but she couldn't bear the thought of Stefan being hurt again. Couldn't stand knowing the serial killer might destroy him while he fought to save her. No. That wouldn't happen. Stefan would prevail. He had to.

Julie settled in the chair, her pad on her lap. She sketched his face in half-profile, eyes closed, dark, thick lashes shadowing his cheeks. Upon closer inspection, she saw a tiny scar bisected one nicely shaped eyebrow, dispelling her earlier impression that vampires had no blemishes or scars. Then her heart beat a little faster when she remembered. Only another vampire could leave scars. Stefan had put himself in harm's way more than once. He'd do so again. That was the kind of man she'd fallen in love with.

She looked more closely, noticed an almost imperceptible imperfection in the shape of his aristocratic-looking nose. Had he broken it long ago in some boyhood accident, or was it, too, a souvenir of another vampire fight? She sketched in the tiny details that made him unique then set the pad beside him on the bed. Glancing at her work so far, she realized he'd inspired her in ways her teachers hadn't. Her drawings, simple as they were, were looking vibrantly alive.

He did that to her. The first morning she'd awakened with him in her house, she hadn't wanted to work on restoring that painting. She'd wanted to attack the blank canvas, create something spontaneous and passionate. Something that represented her own maelstrom of feelings and emotions. She hadn't done it then, but the urge was still with her, still just as strong. As strong as her desire to spontaneously, passionately commit her eternity to the man before her.

The artist she'd longed to become was within her, had always been there. It had taken Stefan to come her way, bringing her innate creativity into full blossom.

He looked so young, so vulnerable as he slept, uncovered but for the top sheet he'd apparently kicked off, now tangled around his feet. Long black lashes shadowed his pale cheeks. His sensual mouth was slack, relaxed, yet fully closed as though he were still concealing the only incontrovertible evidence that he was more than mortal.

Julie shook her head, tried to reconcile in her mind the fact that her lover had experienced childhood not as she had, in the nineteen eighties in New Orleans, but long ago, in another world entirely. "Did you spend your boyhood years playing on the cliffs of Normandy?" she asked softly, visualizing the Allied invasion that had stained the beaches below with blood more than thirty years before her own birth.

Of course he hadn't. At least not then. By D-Day, he'd have been a man—possibly fighting with the French underground against the Nazi invaders or...

Julie used her colored pencils to fill in the hills and valleys of Stefan's face, record the high cheekbones and strong jaw, the most minute details of his elegantly set ear, each laugh line around his soft, sensual lips. His neck was thick and corded with muscle, yet long and elegant, paler than his shadowed jaw. A prominent vein—no, that was an artery—lay just under the surface of his skin, its tone darker, blue-red beneath the satiny surface.

Did vampires feed on each other as a matter of course, or did they restrict their diets to mortals' blood except during their mating dance?

There was so much Julie didn't know, but it didn't matter. All that mattered was the inexplicable, irresistible attraction that had brought her together with Stefan d'Argent. She wanted to survive. Wanted a lifetime to learn about the vampire she loved, to share his triumphs and sorrows. She wanted to be his, for all eternity.

Stefan had already lived four hundred fifty years. He'd have been a child in the late 1500s. Standing now, sketching the full length of his magnificent body on a new sheet in the sketchpad, she tried to imagine how it must have been back then, in France. Tumultuous, if she recalled her history correctly.

Julie concentrated on capturing the power as well as the beauty of him. Admiring the well-developed musculature of his upper body that, even at rest, promised great strength and agility, she noticed once more how he slept yet apparently never let down his guard. He'd have learned young to be cautious, she imagined, for suspicion had most likely been the order of the day during his childhood, fed by the Huguenot uprisings. She couldn't conceive of the carnage he must have seen, recalling the Saint Bartholomew's Day Massacre. The Regent, Catherine de Medici, had authorized that butchery.

Julie shuddered. Vampires would have been reviled during that time, feared even more than the Protestants whose blood had been spilled in the streets of Paris and throughout the French countryside. Taking a charcoal pencil, she drew in the shadows cast through the linen on the sleek lines of his body, portraying the way his broad chest tapered to a narrow waist. Thank God the fates had spared Stefan to grow to manhood. To touch her life now, more than four hundred years later.

She admired his magnificent body, caressing him in her mind as she'd stroked him earlier with her hands and mouth. His cock lay at rest against his ridged belly, curving gently to the right, its tip almost nudging the indentation of his navel. Its head, darker than the pale column of his shaft, flared, ending in a perfectly shaped round, apricot-colored crown just a shade lighter than his large, smooth scrotum. Julie took special pains to record every detail…each square inch of Stefan.

Her art might be all she'd have of him. Her only concrete testimony that for a few wonderful days, a very special vampire had touched her life.

No. She wouldn't give him up. Julie closed her eyes, imagined how they'd spend their days—and nights—if she could only persuade him to make her like him. Turn her and take her as his mate.

A beautiful male…one she wanted for her own.

For hours Julie sketched Stefan, first from one angle and then from another, mixing the colors until she got each tone perfect, each shadow at precisely the right depth. As she did, she imagined herself with him, embracing the darkness, taking her nourishment not from the bounty of the land but from another being like herself. Living in a shadowed world cloaked in centuries of mystery.

Living for hundreds of years. She shuddered at the alien thought, then smiled at the sleeping vampire in her bed. If he turned her, she'd be living for centuries, not decades. Living with him. Loving him. Bringing up a vampire child if they were blessed. Concepts she'd have found incredibly bizarre before he'd come into her life now seemed very possible…desirable.

"What has you looking so serious?" Stefan's sleepy, husky voice drew Julie out of her daydreams, back to the here and now.

She closed her sketchpad and set it on the edge of the bed. Standing and stretching out the kinks in her shoulders and arms first, she returned the pencil she'd been holding to the box with all the others and looked his way. The curve of his back drew her eye as he sat in the middle of the bed, legs apart, one knee bent slightly more than the other. The dimmed light filtering through her makeshift shade shadowed the hollow of his throat, his injured cheek. He looked incredibly sexy.

He also looked as though he belonged there on her bed, gloriously naked…deliciously aroused. Julie couldn't resist. Sitting beside him and stroking the strong line of his jaw, she returned his smile with one of her own. "I was thinking…thinking of painting you. I've been making sketches of you while you slept."

With greater interest than she'd imagined he'd display toward her efforts—he'd never struck her as being vain, though he certainly exuded self-assurance—he picked up the sketchpad. When he flipped it open it to the first page, he gasped. And stared, apparently taking in each detail, scrutinizing every pencil stroke of what Julie had thought a reasonably accurate rendition of his handsome features. "I know it's rough, but—"

"No. You're incredibly talented. I've noticed and admired your paintings, including the one here above the bed. It's just…" He hesitated, his emerald gaze still focused on the colored sketch as though he couldn't tear it away. "It's just that I've never seen a likeness of my own face until now."

"I-I don't understand. Surely—"

"I'm a vampire, not a mortal. As I told you before, my eyes are extremely sensitive to light. Looking at light reflecting off a mirror blinds me."

"But you shave. Brush your hair. How can you, if you can't see what you're doing?"

"I can see shadows but not details when I look at my reflection on polished furniture, so I can tell if my hair's too badly askew or in need of trimming. As for brushing it and shaving, I've had years of practice. And I'm eternally grateful to whoever it was that invented the electric razor. It's saved me many a time from spilling my own blood." He smiled then looked again at the sketch. "I had no idea I looked so much like Alexandre."

Julie was struck by Stefan's obvious feelings of wonder, now that she realized he was looking for the first time on his own image. How would it feel, seeing yourself only through others' eyes? *If you persuade him to take you, make you one of his kind, you'll learn.* The voice in her head spoke softly. Not as a warning, but as a bemused reminder of the many consequences that would result if Stefan changed her.

"Your cousin?" she asked, dragging her thoughts back to Stefan's comment. "The one you told me nearly got tried for that murder in Montana?"

"Yes. Alex's reckless streak will be the death of him, his mother always says." With one finger, he traced the length of the half-healed wound on his cheek as if he expected to feel discomfort from touching the same wound on the paper. "Vampires' wounds usually heal quickly. Unless they're inflicted by other vampires. This one looks pretty rough. No wonder seeing it upset Alina when I met with her last week."

"It doesn't look as though it's infected, but it might be a good idea if I cleaned it and applied some antibiotic cream. Because you can't see it for yourself," Julie amended when he shot her a questioning look.

"I don't respond to mortals' remedies any more than I fall victim to their illnesses. From the look of this, though, I think it would benefit from another thorough cleansing."

Chapter Eleven

The sap from the aloe plant on Julie's bathroom window felt surprisingly soothing when she applied it to Stefan's injured cheek. Cool and slick, it seemed to form a barrier he hoped would facilitate the healing process. Even if it didn't, it wouldn't hurt, and it seemed to please Julie to believe she was taking care of him.

While Julie dressed, Stefan tried to reach Claude telepathically. Then he picked up his cell phone and called the other vampire's hotel room. No answer. Where was his young uncle? Just then Noodles began to yap furiously at the front door. "I'll see who that is." His guard up, Stefan hurried to the door, zipping his slacks as he walked. He lifted the little dog in his arms and looked through the peephole.

"It's okay, girl. There's no one there." When he opened the door, he saw it. The white rose, its long stem wrapped in green waxed paper. Reynard's warning. Stefan picked it up, cursing when a thorn dug into his finger, drawing blood.

His blood. He wouldn't allow the bastard to draw Julie's. As if doors would keep the Fox at bay, Stefan slammed it closed. He held the bud at arm's length, the way a squeamish mortal might handle a poisonous viper. His heart, normally quiet, pounded in his chest. Adrenaline rushed through his body like a river of red, life-giving sustenance, suffusing his muscles, flushing his skin.

"What's wrong?" Julie clamped down on her lower lip when she saw the rose. Her eyes widened, and she began to tremble. "He sent it, didn't he?"

He nodded, not knowing what to say, though he knew what he wanted to do. He wanted to throw open the door, snarl a challenge. Make Reynard come to him, fight it out as decent men should, rather than involving the beautiful, fragile creature before him.

"You—I don't want you to get hurt." Her gaze went to his cheek, to the wound she'd dressed moments earlier.

Fear showed in her eyes, dilating the pupils even more than was justified by the dim lighting in the foyer. Damn it, he hated having her worry about him, hated more the necessity of admitting he couldn't deal with one crazed, murdering vampire on his own. "Come here," he said gruffly, holding out his free hand and pulling her into the circle of his arms. "Let's get rid of this. It's time for me to call in the reserves."

He headed for the kitchen, determined to feed the obscenely beautiful flower to the garbage disposal, the way he'd watched Julie do earlier with her banana peel. Jabbing himself once more with a thorn, he shoved the blossom into the drain chute. "Where's the switch to turn this on?"

Julie reached over and turned the water on. "Here." She flipped a switch to the right of the sink, and the disposal started to grind away. She watched as though transfixed as the thorny stem slowly disappeared in a stream of clear, clean water. "I wouldn't have wanted to touch it. Thank you."

"I only wish it were as easy to get rid of the maniac who sent it." Stefan stepped back from the sink.

"We could go away. Far away. You could make me like you...move us through space..." She held his gaze, pleading, offering him forever, however short that time might be.

Stefan didn't want to lose her. Not to Reynard and not to her world of mortals. If he gave in, took what she offered so sweetly... She would no longer be totally helpless against Reynard. They could fly away together, and he could ensconce her behind the dark, cool walls of his castle overlooking a stormy sea, a place where the d'Argent women had gone for refuge over the centuries. She'd be safe from attack from even the strongest of their kind while he—

What was he thinking? What sort of fiend would turn a mortal then abandon her in an alien world while he went back on what might well be a fatal quest? Particularly the woman who owned his heart? Stefan reached out, stroked the skin along Julie's jaw with the pads of his fingers. So he'd have the sensations etched into his mind long after he was gone, he memorized the satiny texture, the sensual heat of her mortal blood pulsing within her flesh. "Because I love you, my darling, I cannot."

For a moment he considered abandoning duty, keeping vigil over Julie in his ancestral home while others pursued Reynard. Denying his honor for his love. But he could not, for if he did, he'd not be worthy of her love...or his own ancient, respected name.

Tilting her chin up, he took her lips and allowed himself to sample what he must not claim. How would he walk away? Storing memories that would have to carry him through the dismal, lonely days of a future without her, he let her carry him away mentally to a place without Reynard, without danger. A place where mortals and vampires might coexist in peace together.

He felt a gentle but stubborn strength in her slender arms when she clasped his waist, drawing him into her as surely as if they were lying naked in bed. Her rapid, shallow breaths tickled his cheek, his upper lip. With her smooth, wet tongue, she traced his lips, enticing him to take her...make her truly his.

"Stop, Julie. When this is over, I'll go, and you'll forget we ever met." But he'd remember. Remember and regret, for the centuries of life that stretched before him—unless he challenged the killer vampire and was destroyed.

"You may leave me, but I'll never forget you." Her eyes widened, as though she'd suddenly realized the meaning of his words. "You—you wouldn't steal my memories. Surely you couldn't be so cruel."

"Wiping out your memories would be a kindness. I wish I could wipe away my own, for they will haunt me..." Stefan almost hoped Reynard would destroy him, save him from the prospect of living on for centuries without Julie. Almost. Preserving her mortality was more important than serving his happiness. To ensure that he must destroy her would-be killer, not be destroyed himself.

The doorbell rang, its shrill tone piercing the silence. Julie's muscles tightened beneath Stefan's hands, and she inhaled deeply, as though drawing strength from the air around her. Noodles trotted toward the door, the tone of her bark more threatening than welcoming. "Stay here. I'll see who's at the door."

She threw an even look at him over her shoulder. "All right, but don't you dare think this conversation is finished."

Stefan had never in his life been so grateful to see his cousin Alexandre—or so annoyed to see Claude, who hung back as though afraid to face him. He glared at both of them. "Don't tell me you didn't see which way Reynard went after he dumped that rose on this doorstep. Damn it, Claude, you should have been able to track him."

Alex shook his head. "Take it easy, cousin. We've known since the second or third of the murders that Reynard can make himself invisible when he wants to. Just because he doesn't often do it doesn't mean he can't. Obviously the bastard had made Claude, and he didn't care to be tailed today. We saw him placing the order with the florist before he vanished. He never came anywhere near Julie's door. If neither you nor I can follow him when he does his disappearing acts, how can we expect Claude to keep up with him?"

Despite the defense, Claude hung his head, stared down on his dark-brown deck shoes. "I fucked up. I'm sorry, Stefan."

Claude's heart was in the chase, and even with his limited experience he'd proven himself a hunter worthy of respect. Stefan ran a hand over his face, got a grip on his anger. After all, it wasn't his young uncle who deserved his fury. He stepped back, waved the two inside. "You did nothing wrong, Claude.

Both of you might as well stay here for now. Come on, I want you to meet Julie."

* * * * *

Louis laughed. His ruse had worked, and he'd lost the d'Argent bastard who'd been dogging his every footstep for the past four days. Not only him but the other one—the one he'd left for dead in Buenos Aires who now looked disgustingly alive. While he lurked, invisible, he watched the florist's boy lay the single white rose at Julie's door. Though he'd hoped his intended victim would answer the door, it was d'Argent who'd picked up the dewy bud. A few minutes later Louis watched the same one open the door again to let in both of his confederates.

Good. So Louis had primed Alina well with his latest letter. She'd taken the bait and sent three of her best out to challenge him. Let them come. Let them all come. He'd destroy them, fling their lifeless bodies across the ocean and deposit them at Alina's feet. The more the better.

But first Louis had to feed. It would take all the strength he could muster to take on three d'Argent pups at once, destroy them, and claim his bloody prize.

* * * * *

Sitting around Julie's kitchen table, they looked like ordinary, extraordinarily handsome young men, Stefan's cousin and uncle. Only their paleness and—in Claude's case—such prominent fangs that no one could help noticing them when he opened his generous mouth, would have made an unknowing observer wonder if they were vampires. She started to offer refreshment, hesitated, then opened the refrigerator door and set out the remaining carton of blood she and Stefan had brought home from the vampire bar.

"I'm afraid you'll have to share," she said, putting a small crystal tumbler in front of each vampire. "Or…"

"Don't even think of offering yourself, *chèrie*." Stefan's tone brooked no argument.

Claude grinned. "Was that a pizza I saw in the freezer when you were getting out the ice? If so, I'll take that. Stefan and Alex are welcome to share the Vampire Delight."

"Why yes. I didn't realize vampires consumed anything else or I'd have offered."

"Claude is one of the few who can. Most of us get violently ill," Stefan explained.

It seemed Julie was learning something new about Stefan and his clan with each successive conversation. "Would you like a salad with it?"

Alex broke out laughing, a booming sound that startled Noodles from her snooze in the corner next to the patio door and had her ears perking up, her expression quizzical. "Our uncle limits his consumption of food for humans to the junk variety. Pizza, burgers, *brioche au chocolat…*"

"Not so, Julie. If you've got the makings, I'd love a salad." Claude shot a quelling look toward Alex, who by then had turned and was deep in discussion with Stefan. "Marisa has taught me I must try more nutritious mortal fare. She loves watching me eat the foods she used to enjoy, since she's no longer able to consume anything but blood."

"What do you expect, Uncle? You only turned your mate, what? Two weeks ago?" Alex asked, a twinkle in his eyes.

"Three. I want us to finish off the Fox quickly, so I can resume my honeymoon."

Stefan cleared his throat. "We want that too. You are to take care, for it would be a tragedy if you got overeager and gave Reynard an opening to destroy you."

So Claude had successfully turned a mortal. That fact didn't escape Julie's notice, but she said nothing as she washed salad greens and cut a tomato into wedges. At the moment she wanted nothing more than to observe Stefan with his cousin and very young uncle, who seemed determined to carry his weight while Stefan and Alex seemed to be making every possible effort to dissuade him from unnecessarily courting danger.

Their friendship was obvious. Julie guessed Stefan and Alex both worried for the youngest of their number, much like a parent might concern himself over the behavior of an exuberant child.

When the timer went off on the microwave, Julie slid the pizza onto a plate and set it in front of Claude, next to the garden salad he'd almost finished. Anxious to be part of the conversation, she took the last of the four chairs around the table.

"Now, Stefan, don't come down so hard on Claude," Alex said, his face so much like Stefan's but for a devilish twinkle in his clear green eyes. "Julie, you've got to make my cousin take life a little less seriously."

Stefan took Julie's hand then glared at Alex. "You would say that. I know no one on earth who takes life less seriously than you. I expect you to take care also. No more heroic machismo like the stunt that nearly killed you in Buenos Aires. We work together from here on, all three of us."

Though he didn't say it, Julie guessed Stefan meant to call the shots, protect not only her but Claude and Alex from the serial killer. *Please, God, let him survive this encounter they were planning with her would-be murderer.* "Stefan, that means four of us. I want to be a part of this too. After all, it's me that Reynard intends to kill."

Alex looked at her then back at Stefan. From the serious expression in Alex's deep-green eyes, Julie guessed he understood much more than Stefan had put into words. He might have been a playful scoundrel, as Stefan had intimated, but it was obvious Alex was no fool. Stefan shook his head, as though to silence Alex, as if to keep him from revealing...

"You must be part of the plan, Julie, as much as all of us regret it." Alexandre reached over, surprised Julie by covering the hand Stefan wasn't already holding. "You and Noodles will be the bait. It's the only way I can think of that we can draw him out. You're the one thing that makes Reynard vulnerable." He shifted his gaze to Stefan, as though offering the opportunity for him to take the reins.

Stefan had no choice but to do so. He'd promised Julie and assured Alina he'd prove himself worthy of the trust she'd bestowed on him to stop Reynard. "We must stay together, make forays out at night, the four of us, so Reynard will know we've chosen to protect you rather than attack him. Except..." Stefan paused, as though he didn't want to finish the thought, "...in the morning, when the sun first rises, when you'll walk Noodles alone."

"I—okay. You say he doesn't often come out in daylight, so I should be safe."

"I'm counting on him to do just that. He obviously has set a timetable he intends to follow. We'll stick to you like glue all night, when the Fox likes to roam. He'll see you alone with Noodles early in the morning. You'll invite him to come home with you for breakfast. When he does, seat him out on the patio, in the sun. While the light won't incapacitate him, it will weaken him much more than the exposure to bright light affects us. Excuse yourself to bring him something to drink. As soon as you're back in the kitchen, we'll come out from hiding and attack him. All three of us."

"Does he know you all are here?" Julie paused, her expression questioning. "Won't he suspect I'm setting him up?"

"I'm sure he knows. And I imagine he'll recognize your invitation as a set-up. But Reynard is an arrogant bastard. I'm counting on him being cocky enough to believe he can take us all on and win. It will be easier for us to fight him in a small private area like your patio, rather than out in the open where we'd be likely to draw spectators. Humans wouldn't recognize his superhuman strength and would likely as not jump into the fight, trying to even the odds."

A shadow crossed Stefan's face, accentuating the fierce determination evident in his expression. It frightened Julie.

Suddenly this was all too overwhelming. Too frightening. Too much to take in all at once. Despite her earlier bravado, it terrified her that she would soon have to face a powerful vampire intent on bringing about her death. A killer who was nearly invincible, so much so that three brave vampire hunters admitted it would take all of them to take him down. And that they'd need to put him at as great a disadvantage as possible if they were to succeed.

She shuddered, though she tried for a courageous smile.

"We're frightening your beautiful lady, Stefan." Alex bared his fangs in a feral grin, an expression that somehow was reassuringly fierce yet mischievous, easing the intensity of the moment. "Let's hit a bar tonight. Let Reynard know his victim's not alone." He looked directly across the table at her. "What do you say, Julie? Claude says you found someplace with vampire action. Let's go take it in."

When Stefan offered his hand again, she took it, found the pressure of his cool fingers warmed her icy palms. Turning her head, she smiled at Claude. As young as he was, he looked determined, serious and practically deadly with the last bite of pizza poised at his lips.

In the three of them, Julie had the best protection she could get. She was certain of that. "Let me go put on my party clothes. You stay here and enjoy your drinks."

"None for me, thank you. I like mine fresh from the tap." Alex looked at Julie then winked. "Besides, I fed just yesterday."

Stefan lifted his glass, his expression thoughtful as he looked at Julie. Then he shifted his gaze to Alex, smiling for the first time since he'd picked up that white rose from her doorstep. "So did I," he said. "Julie has a way of making me ravenous, though." He lifted his glass, as though making a toast. "Drink up. Alina would not be happy if I refused to ensure you both get fed."

"If you'll excuse me, I'll try not to keep you waiting long." With that, Julie headed for her room. She wouldn't give in to fear, and she wouldn't give up on Stefan. Memories of the vampire bar with its sensual music, the jewel-toned strobe lights, the sexual play of the vampire couples flooded her brain. In her room now, Julie rifled through her closet.

There it was, the perfect dress, a flowing silk wraparound confection in muted tones of primary and secondary colors that had reminded her of a Degas watercolor when she first saw it. The sleeveless v-neck bodice hugged her upper body then swirled around her legs to an uneven hemline. It was as if when she'd bought it months earlier, she'd known somewhere deep inside her that she'd find a lover to entice with it, a perfect setting in which to wear it.

Tonight might be her last night to do such a thing, and she was determined to get exactly what she intended. Stefan.

Chapter Twelve

ℬ

Streetlights illuminated the darkness, calling Stefan's attention to the moon. It grew thinner daily, marking the days until it fully waned. A brisk wind blew off Lake Michigan, making Julie tremble.

How could he resist her? The dress she wore was made for seduction. High heels brought her height close enough to his that she could lay her head on his shoulder. He wrapped an arm around her as they walked to the bar, a few steps behind Alex. Claude brought up the rear, a determined protector in the unlikely event Reynard might alter his plan and come after Julie tonight. Stefan kept an ear open, just in case.

"The cycles of the moon have always fascinated me," Julie said. "This is the final phase, where the moon prepares to join the sun and begin the cycle once again. The bridge between the death of the old cycle and the birth of the new. Did you know legend has it that whatever has been learned during the entire cycle or lifetime is distilled and condensed when the moon wanes? Whatever isn't needed is released, loose ends tied up."

"No. I've never studied much astrology." Stefan loved the sound of her voice, the silent promise in her touch when she laid her hand possessively on his ass cheek. "I remember a poem about the moon, though. My mother knew Vachel Lindsey, the mortal who wrote it."

"The Moon's the North Wind's cookie

He bites it, day by day

Until there's but a rim of scraps

That crumble all away.

"The South Wind is the baker

He kneads clouds in his den,

And bakes a crisp new moon that...

greedy...North...Wind ...eats...again!"

"What a lovely poem. I never heard it before." Julie relaxed beneath his arm, against the shelter of his body, her lips curving up at this bit of whimsy.

"It's called 'What the Little Girl Said'. I hadn't thought about the poem for years until tonight. Moonlight becomes you, you know." He drew her closer, absorbed her warmth, her desire—the love for him that she made no attempt to hide. Her hair, caught the dim light, looked like spun gold. He had to touch it, feel the silky strands between his fingers.

"Well, Stefan, it's obvious you're doing more with Julie than saving her from the Fox. I sense another vampire wedding in the works."

Stefan shot a fierce scowl Alex's way. "You're supposed to be watching for Reynard, not making inane observations."

"Can't help it. Not when it's so obvious that you can barely keep your hands off her. Can't say I blame you, of course." Alex laughed, but he dropped back a little. From the intent look on his face, Stefan guessed he was trying to make mental contact with their prey.

Claude caught up to them, measured his pace with Stefan's and turned to Julie. "Don't worry. We won't let Reynard hurt you."

When Julie smiled at the young vampire, Stefan had to rein in his temper. He'd never felt so possessive of a woman before, and that disturbed him.

Everything about Julie disturbed him. Aroused him. He took her hand, ran his thumb over her soft, warm palm. "I believe you've won yourself two more ardent admirers, Julie. Go on ahead, Claude, but keep your eyes open. Reynard might be lurking anywhere." It was greedy, Stefan knew, but he wanted his remaining time with Julie uninterrupted even by those he'd summoned to help protect her. He ignored Alex's knowledgeable chuckle.

Seductive music filled the air as they drew closer to Rush Street and its many clubs and restaurants. He'd enjoy tonight, show Julie a side of himself that he rarely revealed, that he'd never before revealed to a mortal.

The brush of his hip against hers as they walked, slight yet incredibly seductive, made him lightheaded. He'd take whatever teasing Alex and Claude dished out because he loved Julie too much to keep his feelings under wraps.

* * * * *

At the restaurant a few minutes later, Gus greeted them like long-lost friends before pulling Stefan aside. "Reynard tried to get in here last night," he whispered. "Of course I turned him away."

"But of course." It comforted Stefan to know he could count on Gus, and that while they refreshed themselves, they need not worry about Reynard's imminent arrival.

Gus smiled, his voice now at a normal, cordial tone as he addressed the group. "Tonight the music is live. I believe you'll enjoy the band. Their music reminds me of classic New Orleans blues." Gus motioned toward the back room where they'd gone before. "Go on and make yourself at home. I'd take you myself, but I dare not leave the door unguarded now that I know Reynard is out there, somewhere close by."

"I know the way. Thank you for your vigilance."

Tonight the place was full. When he heard Julie's sharp intake of breath, Stefan scanned the room. It didn't take genius to figure she'd noticed the pair of Callicantzaros, Greek vampires whose swarthy coloring and long, wicked-looking talons set them apart from others of their kind. "They're different from most made vampires," he told her once they'd settled at the table near the dance floor. "Legend has it they come from people who were born between Christmas and

Twelfth Night. It's said that once a year, between Christmas and the Epiphany, they attack their victims and tear them up. They're harmless the rest of the year, so you can relax."

"They look so fierce, I was frightened for a moment." When Julie smiled, she warmed Stefan's heart. "Look, isn't that Alex making friends with that redhead at the bar?"

Stefan laughed. "I'd worry about Alex if he weren't hitting on some female. He has ever had a roving eye for beauty. Do you see Claude?"

"He's down there at the end of the bar, nursing a draft and scanning the room as though he expects Reynard to barge in at any minute."

"Yes, that's Claude for you." Earnest, always eager to do his job, in the way of those who were very young. "He won't be cruising for female companionship, not with his beautiful bride waiting for him back home."

"It seems as though he takes his job seriously," Julie said. "Unlike your cousin."

"Alex likes to joke, but he's deadly serious when it comes to destroying Reynard. So serious that I worry he'll do something foolish, such as confronting him alone."

Julie reached up and brushed her fingers across Stefan's injured cheek. "The way you did in Atlanta?"

"I guess so." He smiled "We're all getting a little reckless. Desperate's the word." No one who'd ever seen one of Reynard's victims could feel otherwise.

Her jerky little smile reminded him she knew she was Reynard's next intended victim. Maybe if he changed the subject, her fear would dissipate. "See that couple in the corner?"

"I see you're trying to distract me. And I love you for making the effort." As though proving her words, she looked over and noticed the two he'd mentioned, their shaven deep mahogany heads and the primitive pale wooden jewelry that adorned their ears and noses so striking as to command Julie's attention. "Oh, my. I'd love to paint them. I can imagine them dressed in African tribal garb—or nude. Are they vampires too?" she asked when she turned her gaze back to Stefan.

"They're Owenga. Reincarnations of ancient evil sorcerers who are still feared by some native tribes in Africa. If they were ever evil, though, it was centuries ago, for now they're among the most highly respected of all the vampire clans."

Julie smiled. "I'd never have guessed if I'd seen them on the street."

"Like mortals, vampires come in all shapes and sizes. All colors. Look. Here comes the waiter with our drinks."

Julie smiled at the waiter then took a delicate sip of her wine while Stefan sampled his frosted stein of blood. She watched him, her expression pensive, and he knew the direction of her thoughts, even before she spoke. "There's no chance we will ever share the same drink? None at all?"

Stefan tried to hide his frustration that she wouldn't let it die. No matter how they both wished otherwise, it must. "None, my mortal darling. Let's enjoy the time we have and not reach for more." He reached over and took her hand.

For a moment sadness shadowed her face, but she quickly managed a courageous smile. "Well, I guess I'd better enjoy you while I can. Shall we dance?"

Stefan wanted nothing more than to hold her, not just now but forever. Still, the idea of trying to turn her and losing her as he had lost Tina, steeled his determination to resist her pleas. "I'll take any excuse I can get to hold you in my arms." Standing, he held out his hand.

Strobe lights accentuated the colors in her dress as it swirled around her slender legs. Red, purple, indigo, blue, green and yellow hues, mingling and merging with her movements, reminded him of the rainbow that often followed fierce storms. The curve of her spine entranced him when he splayed his fingers over that supple flesh. Each delicate indentation between her vertebrae would remain in his memory, torture him in his future as it entranced him now.

He pulled her close, so close that the hard nubs of her nipples brushed his chest and her flat belly cradled the erection he couldn't have willed away if he'd wanted to try. The sway of her body matched his, a perfectly choreographed dance of seduction he couldn't, wouldn't deny.

He imagined her in his castle, in the room where he'd been born, turning from the window to him, love shining in her eyes. She'd have on this dress for a moment longer, until he took her hand, pressed it to her heart. Then the dress would fade away as if by magic. She would come to him, offering herself for his pleasure. He'd be naked too. No pretense, nothing held back. He'd rake her with his gaze, take in every curve of her flesh, the angles of her hipbones and shoulder blades and the indentation of her navel. Although the pulsing vein in her neck would attract him, he'd take much more. He'd make Julie his, his for all time. His for eternity.

A bright flame would flicker in the fireplace, warming the room, heating his blood. He'd take her, lift her into the huge four-poster bed where he was born. For a long time he'd sit beside her, stroking her pale golden skin, tracing each delicate angle of her bones, following his caresses with the gentlest nips of his teeth, the soothing balm of his tongue.

When she writhed against him, overtaken by passion, he'd kneel between her legs and enter her gently, for she was precious to him. But she wouldn't want gentle for long. Her nails would dig into his back. Her little open-mouthed kisses would turn to demanding bites to his shoulders, neck and lips.

He'd answer her in kind, with harder strokes, wilder kisses, rougher stimulation of her most sensitive flesh. He'd claim her. Make her his, forever in the darkness of the night. His for all time.

Pressure built inside him, demanding release. Driven by emotion, not reason, Stefan bent his head to the enticing vein that throbbed beneath the silken skin of her throat.

"Stefan, the music has stopped." Julie looked at him and smiled, the smile of a woman who knew she had stolen a vampire's soul.

That look of utter adoration made him pause, raise his head. He forced himself to remember that look on Tina's face and to recall how she'd looked afterward, her lifeblood drained. Still and pale in eternal death, lying in her coffin in a silk and velvet gown, empire-waisted like the ones Josephine always wore. The brand-new dress Stefan had commissioned from a local seamstress that was to have been Tina's wedding gown. "Yes, my darling, the music has stopped."

No matter how much they both wanted it, he wouldn't take the risk of that happening to Julie.

Chapter Thirteen

❧

She'd almost gotten exactly what she wanted. But she realized now that she couldn't entice Stefan to turn her in a haze of vampire passion. If there was to be a lifetime commitment between them, it must be a mutual, rational decision.

As she must with the impending confrontation with Reynard, she had to have faith in the outcome. Goodness and love had to prevail, and if evil defeated them, she'd hardly be around to worry about it. When Stefan motioned for Alex and Claude to join them at their table, she put on a happy face, smiling despite the uncertainties of her future — and her life.

"Tell me about some of the people here. Please." If she sounded a bit desperate, if Alex and Claude's striking green eyes were too knowing, Stefan's too full of concern, they wouldn't say anything about it. They'd pledged to take care of her, and she trusted that they would.

Alex leaned back in the booth, stretching a companionable arm behind her, winking at her when Stefan scowled. "Let's let Claude tell you about the old guy over there. Come on, Claude, I see you trying to stifle a grin." Alex looked toward a May-December couple fawning over each other in a darkened corner.

Even in the dim light, Julie saw Claude's sheepish expression. "I couldn't," he said.

"It's all right, Claude. I promise not to take offense." Stefan turned to Julie, squeezed her hand. "Claude sees the source of a legend that's caused us all some embarrassment over the years. Since that source was my only sister, I've been known to take offense when the tale is told with too much relish."

Claude looked first at Alex, then at Stefan. "You're sure you don't mind?"

"Positive." Stefan's tone was indulgent.

Clearing his throat, Claude leaned back in his chair like the other two men, apparently endeavoring to appear equally relaxed. "Over in the corner with a luscious *dhampir* beauty, you see the Count of Sainte-Germain. According to the tales I've heard, he was turned in eighteenth-century France when he began to approach old age, but no one knows for sure which vampire did the deed."

"Come on, Claude, I'm sure Julie wants to hear the whole story," Stefan said, a twinkle in his eyes.

Claude didn't seem too sure of that, but he managed a weak grin. "All right. According to legend, the count became a vampire at the hands—or rather the fangs—of a d'Argent black sheep."

"A black ewe, don't you mean?" Alex asked, chuckling.

Claude glanced at Stefan, apparently hesitant to say more. "Of course you're right." He turned to Julie, a shy grin on his face. "It was Stefan's half-sister, Marie-Louise."

"Well, come on, don't hold back all the gory details." Stefan was obviously trying to put the diffident young vampire at ease.

It seemed to be working because the worried look on Claude's face began to fade and he spoke with increasing confidence. "It was a cold winter night in Paris. The year was 1705, and the court was frolicking at Versailles. The Sun King's rule was slowly coming to a close. Marie-Louise was one of the court's most sought-after ladies, for as all vampires do…"

Claude paused, shot a knowing glance Stefan's way. "…she possessed enormous sexual appeal. She also had a voracious appetite for fucking and a nasty habit of seducing mortals and changing them, often against their wills. Marie-Louise took a fancy to the Count of Sainte-Germain, even though in mortal years he was close to death. The way Maman tells it, Marie-Louise seduced the elderly count, turned him and consigned him to a life-in-death of wandering when she died a few months later."

"What happened to Marie-Louise?" Julie didn't recall Stefan having mentioned having a sister, in fact she had the distinct impression he'd been an only child.

"She seduced him, turned him and became his mistress, only to be staked and destroyed by the Count's infuriated daughter. The woman was afraid her inheritance would be compromised if Marie-Louise bore him a son."

"If it had been me, I'd have chosen another way. To stake such a lovely breast…" Alex shook his head, as though the mere idea were unthinkable.

"Crass pig," Stefan said mildly.

"But what other way is there?" Julie asked, curious despite herself.

Stefan stroked her hand. "Staking is one almost certain way of destroying a vampire. Almost certain, because the stake must be driven squarely through the vampire's heart. Two surer methods are carving out the heart or beheading, neither of which is easy to do unless the would-be victim has already been staked."

Julie couldn't hold back the little cry that escaped her lips. "I've always heard vampires would burn if exposed to sunlight. Or die if someone shot them with silver bullets."

Alex laughed. "Those are legends, not fact. I tried the silver bullet route with Reynard. Just ended a two-month convalescence for my fruitless attempt to end his evildoing. Sunlight toasts some vampires but not as thoroughly as you might imagine. First the vampire hunter must lure a highly sun-sensitive villain into the sun and stake him there, because it takes many hours for the sun to do its job."

"Some even say vampires will die if drenched with garlic-laced holy water, or if a killer steals the sock off a vampire's left foot," Claude put in.

"His left sock?" Julie liked the young vampire who obviously held his much older nephews in high regard.

"Yes. There are countless myths as to how best to destroy vampires." Stefan paused, laid a hand on Julie's knee. "And then there are the folk tales of how one may identify a vampire, such as his or her irresistible sex appeal. It's also been said that vampires are repelled by roses, but we all know that in Reynard's case, this is not true. Actually, I like roses myself, as long as they're not white. Many of the myths are based on what's true for one vampire or a vampire clan. Born vampires are less susceptible than made ones to the more exotic methods of detection and destruction."

Alex chimed in when Stefan paused. "Let's see. All vampires have fangs, some more prominent than others, much like mortals have teeth but some are straighter than others. Not many of us have an appetite for what mortals eat or the ability to eat it, and those who do still must feed regularly on fresh blood—but Claude here can manage to feed on raw red meat instead, if need be. I guess all of us could sustain ourselves that way if we had to, but I've never tried it." Alex paused, gestured discreetly at the couple on the dance floor. "I'll bet the male over there belongs to the Sainte-Benedict clan. See his red eyes?"

If Julie had her way, she'd have a long, long lifetime to learn vampire facts and legends. Right now, though, she wanted to spend what might be her last hours with Stefan—alone. "So I couldn't count on repelling all vampires by putting on a crucifix or using garlic juice for my perfume?" she said, trying to push down the selfish thought and match the lighthearted tone her companions had set.

"No. For you I'd risk burning—that's what the crucifix is supposed to do to vampires—and I'd learn to love the stench of garlic." Alex took her hand and brought it to his lips while Stefan rolled his eyes. "Tell me you're not so besotted with Stefan that I don't stand a chance."

"Hands off, cousin. The lady is mine. Until the Fox no longer threatens her." Stefan looked toward Julie, and when their gazes met and locked, she realized he might have read her mind. Or perhaps it was simply what he wanted too, to be alone with her for what perhaps would be their last night together. "Come," he said, his voice deep with desire. "We all need our rest if we are to face our enemy in the morning."

The lady is mine. If only Stefan hadn't qualified that declaration. Julie managed a smile, then stood and waited for her escorts to surround her in the cocoon of their protection.

On the way home, the sliver of a moon seemed smaller, as though moving even now toward the crescent—toward her demise unless Stefan and his friends could prevent it. Suddenly she felt chilled, though the night was unseasonably warm.

* * * * *

Though Julie tried, she hadn't shaken the sense of melancholy—not fear, for she trusted Stefan and his clansmen to protect her—but a deep sadness that portended imminent loss and loneliness.

Despite their connection at the club, Stefan had withdrawn from her once out of its ambience and back at her home, the arena where their last confrontation with Reynard would come. Even now he sat at her kitchen table with Alex and Claude, apparently discussing the strategy they'd use to defeat their enemy. She'd wanted to stay with them, but Stefan had shooed her off to bed as though she were a child who must be sheltered from the fight that was to come

While she appreciated his understanding that she wouldn't enjoy hearing all the gory details, in the back of her mind, she realized Stefan would draw out the meeting with his fellow hunters because he feared being alone with her tonight.

She desperately needed him here, with her, as he'd been the past few nights. She needed him in her bed. Staring at the rumpled covers Stefan had kicked away this afternoon, she pictured him there. Magnificently naked, fully aroused, holding out his arms...holding her. Skimming his large hands over her body. Making love to her as only he could.

She'd stroke his broad, muscular chest, loving the cool, satiny feel of his skin under her seeking fingers. Slowly at first, then faster as he became aroused, his heart would start to beat perceptibly. His cock would grow and harden, and she'd kneel and take it in her mouth, licking and sucking as he groaned with pleasure. Consuming him, claiming him.

His big body would tremble with the effort of holding back, and he'd make her give up her prize. He'd lay her on the bed and take her mouth, her ass, her pussy. He'd claim her every way a man could claim a woman, until she was limp from coming and coming and coming. Then he'd give her a vampire kiss.

And make her his own for all eternity. Julie imagined the sting of his fangs, the ecstasy of surrender, waking later in his arms, transformed.

But he wasn't there. And she believed him when he'd said he wouldn't turn her. The bed she'd loved when she bought it now seemed too large. Too empty. Too full of memories.

Memories she wouldn't let him steal. Julie stood, took her sketchbook and sat on the chaise by the window. If he left, she'd always cherish the look of wonder that had crossed his handsome face when he'd seen it for the first time. She'd remember the exuberance with which he'd played with Noodles on her patio. Most of all, she'd hold on to the myriad emotions he'd coaxed from her, from the moment he'd risked his life to save her dog.

Stefan had stolen her heart. She wasn't about to let him give it back. Some way, somehow, she'd find a way to mitigate his fear. She'd follow him to his world, make it her world too. Her heart wouldn't let her walk away, not when there were so many things they hadn't done together, so many experiences she longed for them to share.

Before Julie saw Stefan she sensed his presence, felt the welcome coolness of his fingers when he laid them against her collarbones and rubbed in a light, circular motion. He wasn't breathing now, or his exhalations would have tickled the sensitive spot where the back of her neck met the base of her skull.

With him touching her like this, the moon seemed to grow brighter. The vanilla scent of the candle she'd lit earlier became richer, fuller. In the silence of the night she heard their heartbeats—his slow, hers racing as she became aroused by no more than the nearness of her vampire lover.

She turned, lured more by him than by the moon. Lifting her hands, she touched his cheeks, tracing the high cheekbones, the strong jaw. Though she'd switched off the lamp in favor of candlelight and darkness shadowed his face, she saw his features in her mind. "You must never steal my memories," she whispered, dragging him to her so she could savor the smoothness of his lips on hers.

His long, thick cock stirred against her belly, strong, insistent. Knowing he wanted her made her inner muscles contract, her pussy grow damp with anticipation. She reached between them and stroked him, enjoyed a heady sense of power when his balls tightened and his cock grew even larger and harder beneath her fingers.

"Fuck me, Stefan. Please."

As though she'd stolen his will to resist, he sighed, lifted her and laid her on the bed. Slowly, as though he relished the unveiling as much as the prize within, he unbuttoned her robe. He bent over her, brushing his lips over each inch of skin he uncovered. "You will have your sketches, my darling, but I'll take this with me—the sweet smell and taste of you, the sounds of your pleasure when you come."

He slid the robe off her shoulders and raked her from head to toe with his beautiful sea-green eyes. "No day will ever dawn without me remembering you. Wanting you." He paused, as though struggling to regain the self-control she wished he'd relinquish just this once. "Never doubt I love you. I can't bear imagining my life without you in it." His expression bleak, he stood, his gaze steady on her as he took off his clothes and came back to her. "This is for now. To leave us both with memories you'll someday wish you had let me erase."

Making memories. Julie concentrated, not wanting to miss a single sensation. The cool yet incredibly arousing touch of Stefan's smooth satiny skin on hers, the taste of his smooth, clean flesh on her lips. The solid weight of his ridged belly against her softer flesh attested that he was real, not some erotic figment of her imagination. Her skin prickled with sensation when he swept his hands along her arms, her shoulders, when he stroked the column of her throat and cupped her jaw.

Wanting more, she opened her legs farther, inviting him in.

He shifted, bringing the heat of his cock to her sopping cunt, barely joining them. "Wrap your legs around me." The order was no more than a whisper against her lips, but when she complied, he surged forward, filling her completely.

How could the rest of him feel so cool while his cock seared her pussy with its heat? Slowly he withdrew, only to thrust into her again. Each time his strokes grew deeper, harder, more intense. Scorching, as the passion between them spread like wildfire. His pubic bone stimulated her clit. The pressure inside her built, spread... She was about to come, but she wanted to make him come first.

Tightening her inner muscles, she milked him hard, spurred on by the ecstatic moans that escaped his mouth. His muscles tensed, reminding her of his strength, her helplessness in his arms. The arms of her beloved vampire.

His mouth opened, flashing fangs.

Yes. He was going to do it. Julie arched her back, giving him better access to her vulnerable throat. She squeezed his cock harder, moved beneath him, with him. Waves of incredible pleasure washed over her when he let go, bathed her womb in hot, staccato bursts that spread throughout her body.

"I love you," she gasped when she felt his fangs graze the sensitive skin of her throat. "Yes, Stefan. Do it. Bite me now. Make me yours." She closed her eyes, let her orgasm take her while somewhere deep within her mind she anticipated quick, sharp twin pains. A time in limbo. Her eventual rebirth as his vampire mate.

But he jerked his head away. "I love you too." He sounded tired…drained…and infinitely sad. For a long time he held her, his head cradled against her breasts.

A tear dampened her skin. And then another. Vampire tears.

Julie ran her fingers through Stefan's dark, shiny hair, as though that might soothe his pain away. "You know, I should hate you for refusing to give me what I want more than anything. But I can't help loving you."

* * * * *

Early the next morning Julie dressed, leaving Stefan sleeping until she was ready to take Noodles for her walk. He looked so peaceful, she hated to wake him—but then, she knew he needed the time to set a trap for Louis.

Still, she sat on the edge of the bed for a long time, watching him, wishing… No, it wasn't the time for indulging in wistful fantasies. Not now, when they soon would have to face a killer. "Good morning," she murmured, bending to plant a hard kiss on his lips.

His eyes opened. Their gazes met. Awareness flowed between them, as if they both realized there was nothing left that needed saying. He lifted her hand and brushed his lips across her palm, a gesture somehow more intimate than the traditional kiss bestowed on the softer back of her knuckles. "We will not fail you, Julie."

"I know you won't."

He rose immediately, fully awake and alert. "Go now. I'll alert Alex and Claude. Remember, you're to bring Reynard in through the patio so we can attack him there. We need the advantage of sunlight."

"But sunlight's your enemy too."

"Not as much as it's his. He'll be in agony by the time he arrives here, and I doubt you could lure him back outdoors if you brought him in through the house. I'm sending Claude to watch you from a distance. He'll signal Alex and me if things aren't going according to our plan. Be careful, my darling. You deserve a long happy life, not the horrible death Reynard has planned for you."

A long happy life. Stefan's words rang in Julie's ears long after she and Noodles went out to set a trap for Reynard. A long life with Stefan?

* * * * *

He'd deal death in the daylight. Something he'd not done before, yet it appealed to his sense of drama since he'd gone to great pains to make his d'Argent pursuers think he was even more sun-sensitive than he actually was. Louis slathered his face and hands with sunscreen designed for infant humans. Digging into his luggage, he found a white long-sleeved shirt and light khaki pants he'd bought because they reflected the sun's light. Once dressed, he donned a hat and dark glasses before venturing out of his hotel room.

The overcast sky was a pleasant surprise. A good omen. The sun lay low, barely peeking from the horizon, looking almost as though it were rising slowly from the depths of Lake Michigan. His skin prickled from the light, but a brisk breeze off the water kept him from suffering excruciating pain. Julie would be walking that nasty little dog any minute now.

There. She let herself out through her patio gate and took off toward Lincoln Park.

Louis followed her, taking care at first in case one or more of the d'Argent pups had made himself invisible to try and trick him. They wouldn't succeed. Louis could feel the presence of other vampires, particularly ones younger and less powerful than he. His senses on the alert, Louis approached Julie, slowly until he was certain she had no invisible guardian.

As he always did in the hours before a kill, he focused on his victim. Unlike the others, this one had undoubtedly been warned and knew his intent. She'd be expecting him, and on some plane that fueled his passion. Three d'Argents guarded her, thought that together they could take him down. The stupid pups! They were so confident, they'd set up the victim to be Louis's bait. They'd soon learn the folly of their plan.

Louis allowed himself the luxury of anticipating the kill, hearing the rush of Julie's blood. He could almost smell her scent—her fear. His fangs itched for the sustenance of her blood, for the revenge he'd vowed against Alina and her miserable clansmen.

He'd hoped she'd have taken that obnoxious dog of hers to walk in the shady park, but no. She chose to stroll along Lake Michigan instead, where the early morning sun was slowly roasting him despite all the precautions he'd taken. Adjusting his hat to shade his face as much as possible, Louis fixed his features to look benign.

Time to overtake his victim. He walked faster. "Fine morning, isn't it?" he asked once he reached Julie's side.

"Why, yes. It is." Julie sounded cordial, but Louis sensed her apprehension. Her d'Argent lover had undoubtedly persuaded her that he, Louis, meant her great harm. "Could—could I offer you coffee? I feel bad that we haven't been able to get together."

It was going to be even easier than Louis had hoped. As he'd gathered, the arrogant bastards indeed were using Julie as bait. They wouldn't succeed, though. Louis was too smart not to catch on, too wily to walk blindly into what might mean his destruction. He knew what he'd face, felt confident he'd prevail. "I'd appreciate it. The hotel's fare is not to my liking."

It seemed that every minute the sky grew brighter and his skin grew hotter. But Louis wouldn't back off. He'd take Julie up on her offer, but being forewarned, he'd be ready. Ready to destroy the d'Argents as well as his chosen victim.

Venom surged through his body, but he made no effort to stop it. It didn't matter now that the whites of his eyes were turning red, or that he was sprouting a tail—actually, more a bump at the base of his spine than a real tail. Julie wouldn't live long enough to notice, once he'd dispatched the d'Argent pups. "I believe your dog has finished its business," Louis said. His strength would be short-lived if he had to remain out in the sun much longer.

Julie's shudder at his touch convinced Louis he was right. The D'Argents would attack him the moment he set foot in her pleasant townhouse, where one of the arrogant pups had passed each day since coming here. "Come, I feel a real need for the refreshment you offered."

Chapter Fourteen

ஐ

"Here they come now," Claude whispered from his vantage point atop the ivy-covered brick wall that surrounded the patio. "He knows we're here."

Stefan fingered the rowan stake, checking its point for sharpness. Satisfied, he set it down on a round wrought iron table next to a razor-sharp cleaver he'd appropriated from Julie's kitchen. Adrenaline surged through his body as he and Alex stood on either side of the spiked patio gate, waiting…

Alex flexed his fists, obviously eager for the battle. Claude perched on the wall, hidden from view from the access path by heavy new spring foliage on a branch of a gnarled black walnut tree. Stefan raised his head, caught Julie's scent, the fetid odor of Reynard. A cold, calculating rage—a predator's rage—rose in him. He felt it reach out, join him to the others.

In that moment they were at their darkest, their least human, blood being their only intent. Blood of one of their own. Of evil incarnate.

"Go for his throat." Baring his fangs, Alex stood poised to strike. The seldom-used hinges of the patio gate creaked. Stefan watched the gate inch its way open, saw Noodles leading the way. "Now!" he said as Julie pulled away from Reynard and raced for the kitchen door.

Claude leapt from the wall, colliding with Reynard and bringing him down. Reynard rolled him over, sank his fangs deep in Claude's neck. The flash of a dagger caught Stefan's eye as Reynard's free arm came up in time to fend off Alex's impulsive lunge. Alex dodged away, came at Reynard again as Stefan joined the melee.

He grasped Reynard's shoulders, pried him off Claude. Alex moved in, dodging fangs filled with venom that could kill, coming in low, pummeling Reynard with vicious blows of his fists. Stefan took a glancing hit from Reynard's dagger but managed to shove Claude out of harm's way.

No time to try to help Claude now, for it took all his and Alex's combined strength to grapple Reynard to the dewy ground. From the corner of his eye he saw Julie standing in the open doorway to the kitchen, her expression one of horror. "Get inside," he shouted.

She turned, but Noodles broke free. The little dog sank her teeth into Reynard's leg, earned a violent kick. She yelped. "Noodles," Julie yelled, scrambling forward into the fray.

Stefan cursed as Reynard burst free and lunged for her, but Julie ducked under the arc of Alex's leaping body as he vaulted over her and collided with Reynard, knocking the killer back into Stefan's hold.

He saw a flash of blade. Felt searing pain. Reynard's dagger had hit bone. Stefan gripped his shoulder, saw Julie was still in harm's way. "Damn it, Julie. Protect yourself. Do it now!" She ignored him, dragging Claude from the battlefield, her hand pressed against his deepest wound, Noodles anxiously dancing behind her.

Stefan let go of his injured shoulder, grabbed and held onto Reynard. He'd die before letting the bastard get to Julie. He dodged the killer vampire's lethal fangs while wrestling him for control of the dagger.

"Hold him." Alex raised the stake. "Reynard, you're history."

Reynard flailed about. Stefan hung on. He couldn't let go. Not now. Not when they were so close. "Hurry, damn it."

His aim sure, Alex raised the stake, lifted it high, brought it down in a vicious arc.

Just as Stefan lost hold on Reynard and rolled away, his shoulder in agony now.

Alex's stake vibrated, sunk deep into the earth where their prey had been seconds earlier. "Fuck." Alex wrenched the stake from the ground, charged at Reynard again. "I've got you now, you murdering bastard," he snarled, impaling the other vampire on the sharp point of the stake.

Through his pain Stefan saw it wasn't a lethal hit. Not for a vampire as old and powerful as Reynard. "We've got to stake him again." Stefan struggled to his knees. Had to get a hold on the killer again. Had to take him down for good. There. Got him. "Now, Alex. Hurry, do it."

Alex charged. With lightning speed, Reynard sank his fangs into Stefan's arm, hard enough to break his grip. The bastard spun away as though he didn't even feel the stake buried in his chest, close to his heart if not actually in it. Stefan struggled to stand but fell backward into a growing pool of blood. His own.

Though he, too, had taken several cuts from the killer's dagger, Alex launched himself at Reynard, but his hands slipped on the other vampire's own blood. Reynard let out a piercing scream, a snarl that rang in Stefan's ears. Defeated for the moment, the Fox limped away, struggling to get airborne and wobbling over the carnage.

The sound that came from Reynard's mouth was half-laugh, half-sob. An inhuman, evil sound that turned Stefan cold. "We've fought this one to a draw. I'll encounter you again. If you survive your wounds." Reynard's parting words rang in Stefan's ears before he sank into blessed oblivion.

* * * * *

Claude lay still as death on a cot in the living room, Alex at his side. Stefan slept now, his wounds stitched and cleaned, apparently healing quickly except for the venom they hadn't been able to extract completely from the vampire bite on his arm. Julie sat beside him on her bed in the darkened room, her heart still pounding now, hours after the fight had ended in a draw.

She'd never seen Stefan look so vulnerable. As though he needed the reassurance of her touch, he reached out, laid his uninjured arm along the curve of her hip. "Julie." Her name sounded as if wrenched from somewhere in his subconscious.

"I'm here, my love." She'd always be there for him, if only he'd allow it.

He shifted. A slight smile curved the corners of his mouth, as though he understood through the haze that surrounded his mind.

"Claude." He said it clearly, though his eyes remained closed.

"Alex is caring for him."

"How…have to know. Have to…"

"Hush. I'll go, find out how he fares. You know, you told me you vampires were all invincible." Julie reached up and stroked Stefan's brow, finding him warmer than usual — feverish from Reynard's venom, Alex had said. "I'll be right back."

Claude didn't look invincible at all. He looked nearly dead, his face chalky from loss of blood. Julie met Alex's solemn gaze. "How is he?"

Alex put a finger to his lips. When he got up and went into to the kitchen, Julie followed. Alex held a chair for her. "Sit. You look as though you could use some rest."

"Thank you."

Alex sat across from her. He looked battered too, though he'd insisted his wounds were superficial. "I didn't want to talk about Claude in there. When Reynard nearly killed me a few months ago, my caregivers spoke about my chances in my presence, certain I couldn't hear. I could. It upset me mightily that I couldn't respond and tell them they were dead wrong when they kept saying I was about to die."

"I understand. Stefan is asking about Claude. I told him I'd find out —"

"Reynard damn near destroyed him. Came close to destroying us all." He paused, met Julie's gaze, smiled. "And to think we all figured we could take him. Damn, but he has the strength of ten ordinary vampires."

Guilt slammed into Julie. "If it hadn't been for me, none of this would have happened. Oh God, I'm sorry." She reached across the table, used a napkin to wipe away a drop of fresh blood from Alex's forearm.

"It's not your fault at all. Our cousin the queen dispatched vampire hunters across the globe long before the Fox singled you out as a victim. She charged us with protecting people like you and destroying Reynard himself. So far, we've racked up a pathetic record. So far, you're the only one of his victims to survive, and the bastard—pardon my language—still lives. We'd best go report to Stefan."

"All right."

In the bedroom, Alex looked down at Stefan's deathly pale body, his expression hard and resolute. "That murderer will not survive for long. I swear it. I will chase Reynard to the ends of the earth, if need be, make him sorry he did this."

Stefan stirred, and his eyelids fluttered as though opening them was almost too much of a task. "Alex. Let Reynard go for now. We've found him before, we can find him again. He's broken his pattern. He might come back for Julie. Hot. I'm so damn hot." He slumped against the pillows they'd stuffed behind his head and injured shoulder.

If only Julie could do something. Anything. Anything to help her vampire lover heal from the grievous wounds Reynard had inflicted. She itched to attack that sick, demented killer, hurt him as he'd hurt her lover. And Claude. Those nameless, faceless women.

But she couldn't. All she could do now was love Stefan, tend his wounds and pray he'd heal.

"Is there anything I can do to help him?" she asked Alex.

"He'll sleep for hours, and when he wakes he'll need to feed. You might call Gus at the bar we went to last night and ask him to send over a few pints of O negative."

"All right."

"Claude will need some too—if he comes to, that is." Alex frowned. "Of course he'll come around. He'll survive. He has to. It would destroy Marisa to lose him now, especially since she's carrying his child."

Claude's mate was expecting? A vampire pregnancy must not be as difficult to achieve as Stefan thought. Julie looked through the open door toward Claude, who hadn't made a sound since she and Alex left him. They'd made him as comfortable as they could, cleansed his wounds as they'd done for Stefan. Julie knew how it would tear her apart to lose Stefan. She couldn't imagine Claude's young bride surviving without him in an unfamiliar world...bringing up a vampire child alone. "Isn't there any more we can do? Are you certain a doctor can't help them?"

"No. All we can do is wait. And see that they both get as much blood as they can tolerate."

Julie glanced at Stefan. "I'd gladly give him my blood."

Alex undoubtedly knew of Stefan's determination not to turn a mortal lover—but surely now, when Stefan lay wounded and needed blood... Julie reached out and stroked his fevered brow. Alex stilled her hand, held it between his own scarred, bloody palms. "He won't turn you. Has he told you why?"

"He told me that long ago he tried to turn a lover, and she died. He's said nothing else about her, not what she meant to him or why it haunts him so after all this time."

When Alex stroked her palm with his thumb, he reminded her of Stefan. They shared the ability to project their emotions with a touch, even a frankly assessing gaze of nearly identical, striking green eyes. "It's not up to me to tell the tale."

Julie focused on his face, his expressive eyes. "I know her name was Tina and that Stefan feels it's his fault that she died. Fill in the blanks for me. Please."

"All I know is hearsay, for when it happened, I was a child—still very much tied to my mother's side." Alex looked at Stefan, as if silently getting his permission to go on. "Stefan was younger than I am now, not even two hundred fifty years old at the time. Napoleon had returned from exile in Elba and led the French Army to a resounding defeat at Waterloo. Louis XVIII held the throne. The year was 1815, and Stefan had led a cavalry division against the Duke of Wellington. Many soldiers died in the battle, and more were gravely wounded.

"After the battle ended, Stefan returned an injured captain to his home in the Beaujolais district and accepted the hospitality of the family, whose greatest asset was said to be Christina, the captain's lovely daughter. Stefan fell under her spell, seduced her and fell deeply enough in love to pledge himself to her, even knowing he'd outlive her by centuries. Her father refused Stefan's proposal, having made what he considered a more profitable match for her.

"Convinced that the honorable thing was to leave and nurse his wounded heart, Stefan bade his sweetheart farewell. But she followed him, begged him to turn her so she wouldn't be forced to marry the man her father had chosen. Stefan gave in, in spite of his youth and the fact he'd never turned a mortal— never even witnessed it being done—and took her to his castle on the coast of Normandy."

Julie looked at Stefan, prayed silently for his survival, his return to vibrant health and vitality. "So they married?"

"No. At least I never heard that they did. The way the story goes, Stefan took her to his bedroom, made love to her, and..."

"Go on. Please."

"...at the moment of her climax, he bit her throat and lost control in the heat of passion, draining her blood and her life. The next morning he wakened from a sated slumber to find her lying beside him, not turned but killed. Cold and dead beyond redemption."

Julie shuddered. It was a heavy burden of guilt she must peel away if she was to gain what she wanted most. She looked at Stefan's pale face, imagined that once he'd been as carefree as Alex. The faint lines at the corners of his eyes and mouth must have been evidence of bottled-up pain, not age as she'd first thought.

"He's one of the strongest of us, but this guilt he carries is a great weakness in his soul. He has stayed in his castle for so many years..." Alex glanced at Stefan then continued. "Alina regretted pulling him into this battle with Reynard, but I think it relieved her to have an excuse to force him out into the world again, bring him back to a full and vibrant life. He's a very good man, Julie. The d'Argents need him. We don't have any elders but for our mothers—and they all are vampires made, not born. In their stead we need cool heads and brilliant minds. Stefan has both."

"Alex, how can I make him know I'd prefer death to life without him?"

"I could change you. I know he loves you."

Stefan's eyelids snapped open, as though he'd been resting, not hovering in that no-man's-land between life and death. "If anybody changes the woman I love, it will be me. Go on, my reckless cousin, now that you've satisfied yourself that I'll survive. Return Claude to Paris so his bride and mother may nurse him back to health."

Julie met Stefan's gaze. "Do you think Reynard will come back?"

Stefan closed his eyes, lay silent for a moment before opening them again and meeting Julie's gaze. "No. He's gone to ground to nurse his wounds, somewhere in the mountains, whether the Rockies or the Alps, I can't discern. Alex, we must have managed to inflict some serious wounds on him."

"I'd consider a stake driven into the chest a serious wound, if it were my chest." Alex spoke casually, as though he staked another vampire practically every day. "I don't think Claude will be up to traveling for a few days. His wounds are more than what I'd describe as serious."

If Claude had been mortal, he'd have been dead by now. Julie recalled the pool of blood she'd noticed beneath his unconscious body. "Speaking of Claude, doesn't he need to be fed?"

"I'll go and try to feed him. If he can take some nourishment, he should be able to travel in a few more days. Julie, I'm sure you can care for Stefan's wounds."

* * * * *

Late that night, Stefan woke, his injuries no longer paining him as much. He still felt weak, but he also was ravenously hungry. Julie lay beside him, lending him her body heat. The curve of her hip cushioned his bandaged arm, and despite his pain he was tempted to slide his hand up and cup her generous breast. He inhaled, taking in the fruity scent of her shampoo. Amazingly, since he felt too weak to move, his cock began to harden.

"Julie?"

She woke instantly and turned to face him. Though it was dark, he saw her clearly, read the concern in her expression. "What do you need?"

You. The words Alex had spoken to Julie when he thought Stefan unconscious would not leave him. *The strongest of us, but a weakness in his soul.*

Alex's voice filled Stefan's mind. *"Take what you deserve. What she deserves."*

He was older, wiser than he'd been two centuries earlier. He knew now how to turn a mortal without losing control. What had happened with Tina had been a tragedy — but one born of an ill-fated love. He'd tangled that tragedy in his mind with the earlier loss of his father, creating one deep wound that had kept him in aching loneliness for so long. He hadn't been able to see it until Julie had pried open his heart. Until she'd offered everything she was—past, present and future—to love him, stand by him. To turn away from her would not only break her heart, it would be an insult to the gift of her love. Thanks to his mother's influence during his childhood, Stefan d'Argent was a gentleman who'd never insult a woman.

As they lay together in the dark, the risk of turning her seemed bearable. "I need to feed." He whispered it.

"Feed on me. Please. I want you to. I trust you not to cause me harm."

It would destroy him if he destroyed her. But going on without her, spending centuries regretting his lack of courage was too much for him to bear. Especially now, when she'd shown him real courage by facing down her would-be killer, risking her life to protect Claude with her own frail body. When Julie faced him like this, with fierce determination to change her life and embrace his world, he couldn't turn her down.

He must find his own courage, face the demons he'd dodged for so long. Overcome the tragedy of his past and embrace who he was now.

Stefan knew instinctively that loving Julie was right. "I know you trust me, love, but I must summon the courage to trust myself." He slipped his free hand between her legs, found her pussy wet and swollen. "Ride me. Please."

Not having full mobility should have frustrated Stefan, but it did not. Julie straddled him, poised to impale herself on his erection, moistening the crown of his cock with her slick, warm juices. He reached up and traced the curve of her hip, her outer thigh, his gaze locked with hers in solemn promise...total commitment. He coaxed her to take him inch by inch, until she held his cock fully within her sweet, hot cunt. Though wanted to rush to the release she promised with each caress of her inner muscles on his cock, he wanted more to draw it out. Have her take him, deplete him, so when their climaxes came...

Fuck. He couldn't wait. When she stroked his chest and pinched the small nubs of his nipples, he had to move. Had to claim her fully. "Ride me. Ride me hard and fast. Satisfy my lust and yours. Now and always."

"Oh, yes. Always." Julie gasped for breath as she moved on him. Her face was flushed with passion, her body took on a light sheen of perspiration—for the last time, he thought, trying to concentrate on the pulsating vein in her throat but being distracted by the delicious sensations in his cock...the slapping of her slippery flesh against his balls.

Her eyes shone with passion. With the kind of love he'd wanted all his life. "Let go, my darling. Come inside me. Give me your vampire child tonight."

"I can but try. Chances are it will take many months of diligent effort before I succeed. Perhaps years." Grasping her hips, he coaxed her to move faster yet, and he arched his back to deepen his penetration. Her soft moans of pleasure took his arousal to a fever pitch.

"Yes. I love how you make me feel inside. Don't stop. You feel so good..." Her words trailed off into a series of delighted whimpers as she bent over him. Offering the pale column of her throat. Offering herself.

Despite his injuries, the dominant male within him burst forth. She gasped as he changed their positions, flipped them so she was beneath him. Her thighs spread to accommodate his thrusts, and she entwined their calves. Taking him as he took her. He slid his hands under her neck, arching it.

His release was coming, drawing his balls up tight against his body, making him flush with an unfamiliar heat. His heartbeat accelerated, making speech difficult. He raised his head, laid his fangs against the tender skin of her throat. "Is this what you want, my darling? Be very sure, for once I've turned you, you can never go back to being a mortal."

"I'm sure," she murmured, taking his head in her hands and cradling it. "Come in me, bite me. Make me your mate."

"I'll love you forever. For all the time to come. For an eternity." Stefan whispered the words against Julie's throat as his hot come began to spurt deep within her body. Then, fighting down the terror that still rode him hard, he sank his fangs into her jugular vein and drank his fill.

"My God, Stefan. I'm coming. Oh, yes." She clenched his cock, her inner muscles milking him. "I love you."

Julie had never come so intensely. Never felt so intensely each scorching burst of his seed within her womb. Never before experienced the ecstasy — the sense of being taken, transformed.

She belonged to him. Totally, completely. Passion coursed from him through her to every cell of her body. Violent pleasure, unlike any she'd ever known. "Don't stop." As though her hands could hold him, she tunneled her fingers through his hair, clutching him to her throat while he sipped her lifeblood.

Indescribable. The heightened sensations slowed but were no less pleasurable. A warm feeling of completion began where his fangs pierced her throat, and in the depths of her womb. It spread, the sense of satiated lethargy, staying with her even when he lifted his head and met her gaze with eyes that glowed with emerald fire.

"You'll sleep, my love. When you wake —"

"I'll be a vampire too." Her eyelids felt heavy. Terribly heavy, but she kept them open, gave him a loving smile. "Your mate."

"Forever." Stefan braced himself above her, watched over her as she drifted away, unconscious from the ultimate vampire ecstasy. She looked so pale. So fragile. "Please," he whispered to her God and whatever deities might listen to a vampire's plea, "let me have created my mate rather than having destroyed the mortal I love."

Through the night he held her, a loving, silent vigil while she lay unmoving, her flesh cooling, her heartbeat slowing... Stefan dared not move for fear he'd miss that next heartbeat. His own heart pumped faster with each passing moment as her breathing slowed, then stopped.

She'd waken. She had to. But what if she did not? No. Stefan wouldn't allow...wouldn't even think he might lose her. He laid a hand on her throat, over his marks of possession. The taste of her blood lingered on his tongue and his fangs, taunting him with the knowledge he'd taken it from her. Taken her, for better or worse. His eyelids drooped, yet he did not sleep. If he slept, he might lose her.

Then, as dawn was breaking, she fluttered her eyelids and smiled up at him. "I'm yours now, for all eternity." He'd never welcomed a smile so much, never wanted so much to get on his knees and thank the fates for bringing him his golden angel. His Julie.

When she lifted her head and kissed him, she grazed his lower lip with her small fangs. "Oh no," she exclaimed, looking with horror at the marks he imagined she'd left on him. She looked bewildered for a moment, as if she had no notion what to do. But then she smiled, bent and licked away the tiny drops of blood, applying a bit of suction to the wound. When she raised her head and met his gaze, she licked her lips. "It tastes good."

"You can drink my blood anytime, my darling. As you are mine, I'm yours." He felt surprisingly strong to have so recently been grievously injured. Her blood had healed him, as his would now heal her if she ever suffered a wound.

Stefan loved the timid way she smiled, as though worried that her fangs would show. "I imagine they'll take a bit of getting used to. They look cute, though."

"Thanks. At least I won't be seeing them for myself." As though experimenting, Julie ran her tongue across her fangs. "They seem awfully small to have hurt your lip like that."

Grinning widely, Stefan bared his own fangs, extending them for her to see and then retracting them. "Once you've learned to control the movement, they'll stay retracted unless you consciously extend them to feed. You'll get used to the feeling, learn to control the movement." The fangs were only one small, visible change that had taken place while she slept. Stefan imagined they'd take less getting accustomed to than feeding exclusively on blood, becoming mostly nocturnal, and learning to propel herself through time and space. "I'll help you, my love," he told her when she reached up and ran a finger over her straight, white teeth, a bemused look on her face when she felt the longer incisors. Stefan looked forward to showing her all the qualities that set them apart from humans.

"I don't want…" Her gaze dropped to his half-hard cock, and her pale cheeks turned a bright, well-fed-vampire shade of pink. "…to hurt you…"

"You won't. When vampires bite, it's a voluntary thing. When you suck my cock the way you're thinking about doing, your fangs will remain retracted. Just as mine always do when I'm nibbling on your nipples or clit." Stefan would risk getting puncture wounds until Julie learned to control the action of her fangs, rather than forego the pleasure of having her go down on him. He slipped one hand over her plump ivory mound and found her clit swollen, protruding impudently from her damp, satin-smooth labia, then spread her legs wide and bent to tongue her there. "I'll take pleasure demonstrating how we use our mouths to love each other, in perfect safety." Delicately, he caught her clit between his teeth and flailed it with his tongue.

Her inner thighs caressed his cheeks while he stimulated her. This was the Julie who'd stolen his heart—yet she was not the same Julie she'd been last night. Instead of deep rose, her pussy glowed shell pink against the alabaster paleness of her newly made vampire body. Every vestige of her body hair had magically disappeared, as he'd known it would, leaving her smooth. Like him, yet even softer. Stefan drank his fill, not stopping until she whimpered and shifted her body, offering him more. Giving of herself this morning as she had last night, with full trust, with perfect love.

"Stefan, I want to feel your cock inside me."

He reversed his position and knelt between her legs, rubbing his cock along her warm, wet slit, seeking the haven of her womb once more. "You're my love, my partner." He sank slowly into her welcoming cunt, his gaze locked on hers.

As the morning sun filtered lightly through heavy drapes, Stefan took his vampire mate for the first time. Lacy patterns of dim light danced between them as they moved in an ageless rite of possession. Though he braced himself on his hands, sparing her the weight of his upper body, in his mind he stroked every centimeter of her glowing skin, claiming it—claiming her for all time. Julie arched her neck, a vampire offering sustenance to her vampire lover. No need now to hold back. Hot semen gathered in his balls, his fangs elongated, and he bent his head to accept her selfless gift. She shuddered, her cunt growing wetter, convulsing around his aching flesh, demanding all he was, all he'd ever be. "Now, Stefan. Bite me now. Bite me as you did before."

He couldn't deny her. Not now, not ever. Letting go the control he'd struggled to hold onto, Stefan came. Mindful of her fledgling status, he sank his fangs with care, nipping…

She screamed, the sound one of ecstasy, not pain. When he lifted his head, she found his neck and bit him. Given with love but without the finesse born of centuries' practice, her tentative bite left his heart beating wildly, his body trembling in tandem with hers.

Apparently drained with the intensity of their lovemaking, Julie fell asleep, her hair spilling over Stefan's arm. Her heartbeat, like his, had slowed so as to be nearly imperceptible. He couldn't resist touching her, petting her satiny skin, running his fingers through the fine strands of her golden hair. As a mortal, she'd sat before a mirror and brushed it to a fine sheen. He'd do it for her now, until she learned to groom herself by touch, not sight. Or until he had to go again, continue the hunt for Reynard until he was well and truly destroyed.

"You'll not park me in that castle of yours while you go off chasing that killer again," Julie said, her eyes wide-open now although he heard sleep in her husky voice.

Amazing how quickly she'd picked up a vampire's knack for reading minds. Stefan had a feeling argument on this matter would do no more good than his orders for her to stay inside had done during the fight yesterday. He took her hand, brought it to his lips. "Wherever I go, you shall go too, my darling. Forever." Stefan watched her expression soften.

"Woof."

"Noodles, you can go too," he added when her little dog jumped up on the bed and demanded their attention.

Epilogue

A wedding? Julie always had expected she'd have one someday, but she'd never dreamed the guest list would be divided between mortals and vampires, or that the ceremony would take place in a vampire bar on Rush Street—a place she hadn't realized existed less than a month ago. She'd never imagined she and her bridegroom would seal their vows with mutual vampire bites as well as the traditional kiss.

Two weeks had passed since Stefan had turned her, and she still had trouble keeping her fangs from elongating whenever her body stirred for him. It still felt strange, passing on mortal food and taking sustenance only from blood. She liked it best sipped slowly from Stefan's veins. Today, though, they fed from rich red human blood served in fine crystal stem glasses.

"To eternal happiness, long life, and many little vamps," shouted their friend Giorgio once the obligatory toasts were finished.

Stefan linked his arm through hers, smiled down at her and whispered, "Easy now. Relax and sip slowly, then retract your fangs."

So far Julie liked most things about being a vampire, except the difficulty she still had dealing with her new fangs. But she wouldn't let a little detail like that bother her on her wedding day. Carefully, keeping her gaze on her new husband's, she sipped, swallowed. It wasn't all that hard, sort of like drinking soda from a straw.

The change that gave her the most pleasure was that her skin had become satin-smooth. Not a body hair in sight. Stefan made no secret about liking her even better without it, and it pleased her not to have to endure monthly bikini waxings to keep herself as silky as a newborn baby. Just thinking of him licking and nipping at her pussy with nothing between them to mute the erotic sensation had her wishing they were somewhere private. She felt herself growing damp, anticipating his touch, the glide of his hot, smooth cock along her slit, the delicious friction of private flesh on private flesh.

He looked darkly handsome in his tuxedo, but she loved him best naked, lying back and letting her explore his magnificent body with her eyes and hands and mouth. Whenever he smiled, her mouth watered. She had to struggle to keep her fangs retracted, but so far she'd managed to do it when they indulged in sexual foreplay. God, but she loved giving him oral sex, sucking and licking his smooth, hot cock and balls while he used his tongue to titillate her clit, her cunt...the rear passage no one before him had ever touched that way.

Since she'd become a vampire, her reactions to emotional and sensual stimuli had become more intense. From the first day, she'd found herself feeling and seeing things in more vivid detail. She even found herself entering Stefan's mind, learning his thoughts before he voiced them. Though she now went out only in total darkness, for unlike Stefan she could tolerate almost no daylight, everything seemed bright as long as she had him by her side.

Soon she'd go back to painting. Her new vision shone through in the portrait of Stefan that she'd just completed yesterday. Hopefully she'd find a similar passion in all her art, though she doubted she'd ever surpass that one love-inspired masterpiece. A fleeting regret dulled her happiness when she considered she'd have to paint the matching portrait of herself from memory, or from photos taken when she'd been mortal.

A small disadvantage, knowing now she had a long lifetime to be seen only through others' eyes. Through Stefan's gorgeous green eyes that she hoped he'd pass on to the children they hoped would be theirs.

The back room at *Ristorante della Rubio* had a festive look. Roses in every color but white decorated every table. Candles flickered in ornate standing sconces at each corner of the dance floor. Thrilled they'd chosen his club as the site for their wedding, Gus supervised a dozen waiters, pointing out which guests got the mortal menu and which ones drank only aperitifs made of fresh AB-negative and French sparkling water. A string quartet made up of d'Argent vampires—friends of Stefan's mother—played romantic pieces from centuries long past.

Noodles relaxed on a pillow at Stefan's feet, enjoying the bone from Julie's father's steak. She'd join them on their honeymoon in New Orleans, where the wedding festivities would continue in Julie's childhood home despite the city's decimation last summer from the hurricane and resultant flooding.

Stefan leaned over, whispered in Julie's ear, "Are you happy, Madame d'Argent?"

"Deliriously happy. Anxious for you to meet the friends I grew up with in New Orleans and then to get my first look at our new home."

"That may not be for a while, if Alina's hunch is right. According to her spies, Reynard is still recuperating from his wounds, but he's sent his clansmen on the move. They're charged with going after Alina herself. We'll have to fight them with all we've got." He paused, and when she read his thoughts she knew he hated that their honeymoon would be cut short. "Let's go. I want to fuck you now. I want to feed on you and have you feed on me."

She squeezed his hand. "I want that too. Dare we take our leave?"

"Soon, my darling." He slid a hand up her thigh and cupped her mound through her skimpy satin thong. Bending to her ear, he whispered, "I like your underwear. I like your bare skin more, though."

"If we're going to go, we need to say goodbye to my father." As much as she wanted to be alone with her new husband, Julie couldn't bear to hurt Sam. After all, he'd been the only one she could turn to with her problems since her mother's death when she'd still been a little girl.

Stefan glanced around the room, obviously understanding what she hadn't said. "There he is. Dancing with Alina."

"Really?" Julie had liked Stefan's regal cousin from the moment they met. It had surprised her that the vampire queen so closely resembled her, even though she should have expected it, considering that a crazed serial killer had singled her out for exactly that reason. Her father apparently liked Alina too, because he'd danced with her several times, seemed intent on staying close by when she chatted with Stefan's mother and half a dozen of her friends.

Julie laid her hand on Stefan's wrist. She couldn't take a lot more of his teasing without ripping off her clothes and his, indulging in a frenzied vampire mating for all their guests to see. Vampire compulsion? She didn't know, but she could barely maintain any decorum at all when he persisted in whispering erotic suggestions, strumming the erogenous zones of her body with the skill of a master. Maybe if they talked about mundane things…

"You know, this is the first time since Mother died that I've seen Sam pay any attention to a woman. Do you think—"

"I think I have to get you alone, and soon." He slid his hand between her legs again and slowly thrust a finger in and out of her wet, swollen cunt as he whispered in her ear. "Imagine you're taking my cock. In your cunt. Your mouth. Your incredibly tight virgin ass. Oh, my darling, you're hot and swollen. Inviting me to fuck you here and now. You're soaking my hand with your pussy juices. That's it. Squeeze me." He went silent as she tightened her inner muscles around his finger. "You like the idea of me claiming that last bastion of your girlhood, don't you? Think. Imagine me fucking your ass the way I fuck you here. You'll feel full. Hot. I'm sure you'll wish I had two cocks so I could fuck both holes at once."

"No. This one is quite enough." Determined to get him as hot as he was making her with words as much as foreplay, she squeezed his rock-hard cock through his tuxedo pants. "But perhaps..." She let her gaze circle the room until she found Alex. Giving Stefan a hot look, she wet her lips then glanced back at his cousin. "Perhaps—"

"You'd like for Alex to join us in *ménage a trois*, wouldn't you? Whatever my darling wants, I'll give her. Close your eyes. Let your mind drift." As he spoke he withdrew his finger from her wet, swollen flesh. Then, in sensuous slow motion, he stood and drew her to her feet. Multicolored floodlights that lit the dance floor came into focus on them, the rich jewel tones swirling about, encompassing them in a surreal cocoon. Julie felt as if she were being transported to a world apart, a place where nothing mattered but the two of them. Their clothing fell away by vampire magic as they spun to the accelerating rhythm of the sensuous music.

Soon she was floating with Stefan in an alien world. Naked. Cloaked in her love's warmth as they drifted up and away, seemingly weightless. Stefan's strong hands held her firmly at her waist while he nibbled on her throbbing clit and thrust his agile tongue deep into her cunt while working a finger gently up her ass. *Preparing you to take my cock. So tight. So tempting. Relax now, and enjoy.*

Stefan hadn't spoken, yet Julie heard him in her mind. Basked in his words of love, of sex...of sharing. The heat intensified around them when Alex floated into their private world, as beautifully naked as they. Magnificently aroused. *Give my cousin a proper welcome. You know you want to.* Compelled by Stefan's silent order, Julie reached out, brought Alex's long, thick cock to her mouth and very gently ran her tongue over his plump cock head. She measured his length with seeking fingers, eliciting a throaty groan.

Feels good. Too fucking good. Stefan, I'm not sure I'd share my mate, not even with you.

I'm sharing her with you, cousin, because I love her and she wants this vampire ménage.

Stefan floated away from Julie's swollen pussy, swooped down to bestow a vampire kiss first on Alex then on her. As he fed lightly at her throat, he pressed his hands on Alex's ass, encouraging her to swallow all his cock, to feel the weight of his heavy scrotum against her lips.

For what seemed a slice of eternity they petted her, stroked her, brought her to a fever pitch of need. She had to have their huge cocks in her, filling her, initiating her into a rite she'd never realized until now how much she craved. "Fuck me now!" she cried as soon as Alex freed his sex from between her trembling lips, heedless of the wedding guests who had to have heard. Who must be watching her being fucked not only by her vampire mate but by his cousin.

She found the idea that eyes were watching them incredibly embarrassing. Even more, though, she found that thought titillating. Would the mortals gasp with righteous indignation? Would they all want to join in the orgy of erotic sensation that gripped her?

They moved in perfect synchrony, Stefan to her back while Alex floated beneath her, guiding her down on top of him, his long fingers plucking at her puckered nipples, his cock head hard as stone against her swollen pussy. Stefan growled as he sank his fangs into her throat while he pressed his cock insistently at her rear entry. *If Claude were well enough to be here, you'd be taking him in your mouth.*

When Julie whimpered, Stefan inserted his finger between her lips. *Suck. Now.* He flexed his hips and breached her anal sphincter muscle. It stretched her unbearably, hurt so much she barely realized when Alex mimicked Stefan's motion and filled her cunt with his own cock. "I'm sorry, my love. Relax. Let us fuck you. Let us give you pleasure so incredible you'll forget the pain."

The pain gave way quickly to a sense of fullness. Of brilliant eroticism played in slow motion, in perfect rhythm that built inside her to a crescendo of pleasure more intense than any she'd ever known. So intense it could be endured once in a lifetime. Julie heard a primal scream, realized it was her own.

"Easy, my darling." Stefan's voice, deep and calming, penetrated the fog of her mind.

She looked down at them, found them fully clothed in their wedding finery, not naked as they'd been moments earlier. "Alex?"

"Over there." Stefan inclined his head toward a corner table where his cousin was involved in an animated conversation with Margaret Ammons, one of Julie's childhood friends.

What? How?

"Vampire magic, love. Don't question its power. What do you say we make our farewells and fly away to our nuptial bed? The rest of these good people can make their way to New Orleans without us."

Julie had no intention of doubting vampire power, not when the aftershocks of the most intense orgasm she'd ever had still racked her body. "Let's. I'd like to experience some more of this vampire magic." She had no doubt it would be there waiting, in the bridal suite at the elegant Monteleone Hotel that Alex had booked for them as a wedding gift.

"All right. Your father and Alina just left the dance floor. Come on, we'll tell them goodbye and be on our way." Julie felt Stefan's impatience in the abruptness of his movement as he strode from the dance floor, his hand almost painfully gripping hers as he dragged her along behind him. "Noodles! We can't leave her behind."

Stefan paused beside their table, bent and grabbed Noodles' leash. "Sorry, girl," he growled when the dog let out a yelp.

Before Julie could protest his unseemly haste, Stefan had maneuvered them through the dancers to her father's side.

"We're going to leave now, Sam." Since her mother's death when she was small, Julie had called her big, indulgent father by his first name. She met his gaze, read pride and love—and a bit of lingering concern about the abruptness of her decision to marry. Since she'd introduced the two males most important in her life, Sam had mellowed — after all, Stefan had the persuasive abilities of an old, experienced vampire, and whatever reservations her father had seemed to be gone now.

No doubt, his lack of reservations about her choice of mate also had something to do with Alina. The vampire queen rested an elegantly manicured hand on Sam's arm. "You take care of Julie now," Sam told Stefan before covering Alina's hand with his own. "We'll see you in New Orleans."

"Okay." Julie turned to Stefan and whispered, "Let's go."

Stefan took Julie's hand. "Hold on." A strange feeling came over her, a sense of being invisible. Maybe they were, because they made their way from the reception without encountering any of their other guests. Once outside the restaurant, he lifted Noodles and deposited her in Julie's arms. Then he lifted Julie herself, heedless of her protests that they'd forgotten their luggage.

"Forget clothes. I'll buy you more. Unless I decide I want to keep you naked." Stefan dropped a light kiss on her mouth then took to the air.

Moments later, they landed in the shadows of a New Orleans alley, near their hotel suite.

Stefan set Julie on her feet. "Put Noodles down. I can't wait another moment to taste you."

His fangs grew longer before her eyes. His green eyes glowed, the whites of them and his teeth glistening in the moonlight. She'd never seen him look so dangerous — or so irresistible. Setting her hands on his shoulders for balance, she arched her throat in invitation. One vampire lover, offering sustenance to another. His expression fierce, he lowered his head.

Sank his fangs into her. At the moment of penetration, a sense of contentment flowed between them. Julie slid her hands up, tunneled her fingers through Stefan's glossy dark hair.

"God, how I love you," she whispered as he shuddered with his own completion. "My husband."

"Let's check in. I want more than a taste, Madame d'Argent." They rounded the corner, arm in arm. In an opulent lobby reminiscent of an earlier, less harried age, they registered, Julie enjoying the indulgent smiles from people in the lobby when they noticed her and Stefan in their wedding finery.

In the elevator, he gathered her in his arms, nibbled at her neck. "Did you enjoy our trip?"

"Very much. So much quicker than an airplane. More private too."

He slid his hands up her body, cupped her breasts. "This elevator's private too. And it leaves me free to touch you like this."

By the time the machine glided to a halt on the top floor, Julie could barely wait to get inside their suite and take their erotic adventure to its natural conclusion. Noodles flopped on the cherry-red bath rug while Stefan eyed the huge four-poster bed with its heavy drapes and mosquito netting, no longer necessary now, as the hotel had been air-conditioned for years, but perfect as a makeshift vampire lair. He regarded Julie with a hungry grin.

Julie looked around the luxurious room. Then she saw the basket. Approaching it, she fingered a large glass dildo that caught the light of a fat, fragrant candle. She'd never seen some of the sensual playthings before, but her sex grew damp when she imagined Stefan tickling her clit with the red ostrich plume, working the strange-shaped vibrator into her rear passage. She spied a black leather cock ring, imagined it strapped around her bridegroom's impressive sex.

"See anything you like, *chèrie*?" She didn't see him, but with that sometimes distracting vampire perception, she sensed he'd come up behind her. Close enough that the heat of his passion seared her buttocks. Close enough for him to skim his hands over her back, lowering the zipper of her wedding gown.

Tension sizzled between them. Julie stepped out of the gown then turned to face him, naked except for ivory stockings and a red satin thong. He threw off his tuxedo jacket and toed off his shoes.

"Let's play." His expression dark with vampire lust, he bent and sucked her puckered nipples, first one and then the other.

Julie loved the suction, the heat of his mouth. The slight rasp of his teeth when he gave each hardened nub a playful nip. "Oh, yes."

He glanced at the selection of sex toys and grinned. "We'll try out some of these toys too."

Julie loosened his suspenders and worked the studs from his shirt then slid it off his shoulders. She laid her cheek on his chest, listened to the slow, barely perceptible beat of his heart. It accelerated in perfect accord with hers as he stroked her belly, her mound, her clit that had already swollen and grown hard with anticipation.

The buttons on his pants gave her a moment's pause, but seeing him magnificently naked, deliciously aroused, was worth the effort it had taken to unwrap her prize. She cupped his velvety scrotum with both hands and bent to lick the tip of his cock with her tongue.

"I love you, husband."

"And I love you. Let's go to bed."

The sun was rising over the nearby Mississippi River, peeking through ancient oak trees festooned with Spanish moss, but the lovers didn't notice. They lay in the heavily draped bridal bed, deliriously happy as they consummated their vows. Julie snuggled in Stefan's arms. So happy she was eternally his.

Enjoy An Excerpt From:
Dallas Heat

Copyright © Ann Jacobs, 2003.

For nearly two weeks Dan had pictured Gayla, imagined what she'd wear and how she'd fix her satiny sable hair for the banquet. The reality of her in shimmering deep red silk that hugged every tantalizing inch of her from shoulder to ankles, except for a side slit that gave glimpses of one long, silky leg, nearly took his breath away when she let him into her apartment.

"I'm almost ready. Let me get my shoes. Would you like a drink or something?"

Her smile faltered a little, as if she were no more used to going to the glitzy kind of banquet Frank had sentenced them to for the evening than he was. "I'm okay," he told her, wishing he could get out of this monkey suit, strip off her dress, pull those glittering pins out of her elegantly upswept hair, and haul her into the small bedroom he could see from her living room.

* * * * *

"Do you do this often?" she asked after they had driven into the city and Dan handed his keys to an attendant at the downtown hotel where the banquet was being held.

He took her hand, as much to reassure himself as to guide her. "No. I'm here because someone bewitched the chief of our group into believing we can reel in enough donations here so we can keep helping patients who can't afford rehabilitative surgery or therapy. Given the choice, I'd be taking you somewhere quiet — private. How about you?"

Dan felt Gayla's almost imperceptible shudder as she glanced around the ballroom. "It's been years since I've gone to an affair like this one."

"Smile, princess. We'll make this fun." In the ballroom now, Dan searched for familiar faces. His hand at Gayla's waist, he maneuvered her through the crush of elegantly clad guests, making his way to the table.

Introductions went quickly, and before long it seemed Gayla was right at home with Dan's colleagues. Her self-deprecating humor, the easy way she fit in with the members of the team—the twinkle in her dark brown eyes when she looked at him—combined to help him have fun and ignore the serious reason he'd come.

Gayla squeezed Dan's hand as they walked onto the dance floor. He made being back among the Dallas medical community seem easy. Resting her cheek against the crisp black wool of his tuxedo jacket, she let herself move with him, in time with the slow, dreamy song the combo was playing. She liked the partners he'd introduced as his family, and felt as if she belonged when they included her in their irreverent, shamelessly self-serving conversation about finding donors to placate the hospital and keep their program alive.

"I like your friends," she murmured as she watched Jim and Kelly showing off with intricate dance patterns. "Especially Michelle. Frank doesn't seem comfortable, though." The striking blond who looked more like a pro football player than a doctor had uttered maybe ten words other than when he was wooing a potential contributor.

"This is even less Frank's kind of party than it is mine. Since his wife left and took their little boy to California, his whole life is our rehab program. Nothing other than the threat of losing hospital backing could drag him to a function like this."

"Then he and Michelle aren't…"

"He more or less ordered Michelle to come with him. Since she's part of the group, she had to be here anyhow. Frank swore off women after Erica walked out." Dan increased the pressure of his hand at Gayla's back, and instinctively she snuggled closer.

He moved with an easy, natural rhythm that made her melt inside. With him she felt beautiful…protected from the spirits of her past that she'd thought would haunt her tonight.

As they walked back toward their table, the most fearsome of those ghosts appeared, and it looked as though he was heading their way. She grasped Dan's hand a little harder. Maybe, if she concentrated hard enough, she could call on his strength as well as her own.

"It'll be all right, princess." Obviously Dan was as aware of her father as she was. Gayla wasn't sure if the tension that radiated from his hand all the way to her constricted throat was all her own.

She forced a smile and made herself look at the man she'd idolized—the one who had bitterly denounced and disowned her, she reminded herself when she suddenly had the urge to run to her father and throw her arms around him. "Dad," she murmured when they came within arms' length of each other.

"Newman." Her father gruffly acknowledged Dan's presence but not hers. The lump in her throat grew.

Dan squeezed her hand as if he knew she needed the contact to realize she wasn't alone. "Dr. Harris. It's good to see you."

"It would seem that my wayward daughter has surfaced."

Her father looked not at her but straight through her. When had been the first time she'd turned his stern features icy cold like this? Gayla couldn't remember. All she knew was that this encounter was almost more than she could bear. If Dan hadn't been at her side, an anchor in this emotional storm, she'd have turned and run as far and as fast as she could.

Dan cleared his throat. "If you'll excuse us, sir, we'll go back to our table."

"I want to talk to you, Newman. Alone." Her father locked gazes with Dan, making Gayla shudder again as she turned to walk away.

After she sat down at the table beside Michelle and Frank, Gayla watched her father herd Dan into a secluded alcove. Her father's angry gesticulations and Dan's horrified expression gave her a good idea that she was the subject of the tirade. When Dan came back to the table, he seemed shell-shocked.

"I'm sorry about that, princess. I'd have liked to tell your father we'd have to postpone that talk, but with the power he has as chief of surgery, I didn't dare. Shall we dance?" he asked, his expression so earnest she wanted nothing more than to feel his strong arms around her again.

She couldn't, though. She couldn't put him in a position where her father would want to destroy him. "Please get me out of here, Dan." She tried to suck in a breath despite the excruciating tightness in her throat.

Why an electronic book?

We live in the Information Age—an exciting time in the history of human civilization, in which technology rules supreme and continues to progress in leaps and bounds every minute of every day. For a multitude of reasons, more and more avid literary fans are opting to purchase e-books instead of paper books. The question from those not yet initiated into the world of electronic reading is simply: *Why?*

1. *Price.* An electronic title at Ellora's Cave Publishing and Cerridwen Press runs anywhere from 40% to 75% less than the cover price of the exact same title in paperback format. Why? Basic mathematics and cost. It is less expensive to publish an e-book (no paper and printing, no warehousing and shipping) than it is to publish a paperback, so the savings are passed along to the consumer.

2. *Space.* Running out of room in your house for your books? That is one worry you will never have with electronic books. For a low one-time cost, you can purchase a handheld device specifically designed for e-reading. Many e-readers have large, convenient screens for viewing. Better yet, hundreds of titles can be stored within your new library—on a single microchip. There are a variety of e-readers from different manufacturers. You can also read e-books on your PC or laptop computer. (Please note that Ellora's

Cave does not endorse any specific brands. You can check our websites at www.ellorascave.com or www.cerridwenpress.com for information we make available to new consumers.)

3. *Mobility.* Because your new e-library consists of only a microchip within a small, easily transportable e-reader, your entire cache of books can be taken with you wherever you go.

4. ***Personal Viewing Preferences.*** Are the words you are currently reading too small? Too large? Too… ANNOYING? Paperback books cannot be modified according to personal preferences, but e-books can.

5. ***Instant Gratification.*** Is it the middle of the night and all the bookstores near you are closed? Are you tired of waiting days, sometimes weeks, for bookstores to ship the novels you bought? Ellora's Cave Publishing sells instantaneous downloads twenty-four hours a day, seven days a week, every day of the year. Our webstore is never closed. Our e-book delivery system is 100% automated, meaning your order is filled as soon as you pay for it.

Those are a few of the top reasons why electronic books are replacing paperbacks for many avid readers.

As always, Ellora's Cave and Cerridwen Press welcome your questions and comments. We invite you to email us at Comments@ellorascave.com or write to us directly at Ellora's Cave Publishing Inc., 1056 Home Avenue, Akron, OH 44310-3502.

THE
✟ ELLORA'S CAVE ✟
LIBRARY

Stay up to date with Ellora's Cave Titles in
Print with our Quarterly Catalog.

TO RECIEVE A CATALOG,
SEND AN EMAIL WITH YOUR NAME
AND MAILING ADDRESS TO:

CATALOG@ELLORASCAVE.COM

OR SEND A LETTER OR POSTCARD
WITH YOUR MAILING ADDRESS TO:

CATALOG REQUEST
c/o ELLORA'S CAVE PUBLISHING, INC.
1056 HOME AVENUE
AKRON, OHIO 44310-3502

Cerridwen, the Celtic Goddess of wisdom, was the muse who brought inspiration to storytellers and those in the creative arts. Cerridwen Press encompasses the best and most innovative stories in all genres of today's fiction. Visit our site and discover the newest titles by talented authors who still get inspired - much like the ancient storytellers did, once upon a time.

Cerridwen Press

www.cerridwenpress.com